Praise for Joy Blowing

Watching these two fall in love is the best thing that's happened to UK railroads since Thomas the Tank Engine.

R T Magazine

It sparkled with joy, it overflowed with texture and love and authenticity.

Scattered Thoughts Book Reviews

Well-plotted and well-written, with lovable leads, nosy neighbours, heart-stopping action fraught with danger and...Mabel. This one is a winner and a recommended read.

Gay Guy Reading

The detective work is engaging and the sex between Ryan and Sam is scorching hot. There is a thrilling, lengthy scene of extremely dynamic danger that I could not read fast enough to find out how things turn out. Highly recommended!

USA Today's HEA blog

Blowing Off Steam

Joy Lynn Fielding

This is a work of fiction. Names, characters, places, and incidents either are the products of the author's imagination or are used fictitiously. Any resemblance to actual persons, living or dead, businesses, companies, events, or locales is entirely coincidental.

Blowing Off Steam

Copyright first edition © 2015 Joy Lynn Fielding. All rights reserved.

Second edition © 2017

Chapter One

SAM

Sam wrapped his Marmite sandwiches in greaseproof paper and slid them into the brown leather satchel on the kitchen table. He checked to make sure they were protected by his notebook and wouldn't get crushed by the flask of tea he'd just packed. It had never yet happened, and having been following the same routine for the last thirteen years, ever since he was eleven, he didn't know why he still had to check. He just knew that he did.

Slinging the satchel over his shoulder, he headed out of the front door, turning to give it the extra tug it needed to close after swelling in the recent wet weather. There was no sign of rain now. Early morning sunshine was bright on his face, though the May morning was chilly enough to have him glad of his hoodie. The forecast was for a fine day and he was grinning with anticipation as he turned left at the end of the street and headed for the railway station.

Val was the only other person around this early. She was straightening the timetables in the rack next to the ticket counter while trying, unsuccessfully, to suppress a yawn.

He'd nearly made it safely past when she spotted him. "Hi, Sam," she chirped, all evidence of sleepiness disappearing.

"Oh, um, hi," he said, attempting to sound surprised and as if he hadn't seen her there, despite her low top and short skirt that had most of the customers checking her out either in disapproval or appreciation.

"Your day off?" she asked, somewhat redundantly, Sam thought, because he *always* had Tuesdays and Wednesdays off. And it wasn't likely he'd be haunting the station if he was supposed to be at work. Before he could answer, she'd moved on. "So what did you get up to last night? Another exciting night talking about trains with your online friends, I bet. You should come out sometime with me and the girls so we can introduce you to guys who don't spend their lives hiding behind computers."

God, no. Just the thought of Val and her friends in all their giggly, flirty glory was bad enough. Once they had a few drinks inside them, they'd be unstoppable. His insides curled up in terror. They already looked him up and down like he was a piece of meat—or at least, they had ever since he'd started working out two years ago and added some muscle to his gangly frame—and the thought of them shoving him at some guy, undoubtedly straight, who'd probably punch him...

"That's okay, thanks," he said, already moving.

"But, Sam—"

"Gotta go. The London express is due!"

He didn't *quite* run, but his heart was still pounding fit to burst by the time he emerged onto the sunlit platform and made his way up the steep flight of stairs onto the footbridge that crossed the tracks. He'd need to avoid the ticket office for the next few days, till she'd got another victim in her crosshairs.

In the meantime, he hadn't been lying—the London train was due in three minutes' time. He walked across the bridge until he was standing over the middle of the track down which it would come. And he stood and waited.

He heard it before he saw it. When it became visible in the clear air of early morning, it looked like some mythical dragon with sun glinting on its metal hide as it wound through the countryside and rounded the long curve into the station. He grabbed at the handrail on the bridge as the train thundered down the track towards him. Although he knew it had slowed for safety reasons, it was moving with such force, such power, that it seemed it was coming at him like a cannonball. It swept beneath him, and the deafening sound it made and the smell of diesel left hanging in the air after it had passed were the most perfect things in the world. Its speed and noise had the footbridge trembling slightly, and he knew how it felt—there was something about that much power that left him weak-kneed and gasping.

As he stood there, slowly recovering from a rush that was like nothing else he knew, he caught sight of a familiar figure sauntering along the platform he was headed for. His hands clenched tighter around the rail as he watched. The London express wasn't the only thing that had him feeling weak at the knees these days. Ryan Saunders had only been here seven weeks, but they had been the seven most tantalising weeks of Sam's life.

Ryan Saunders was not only the living embodiment of every single one of Sam's fantasies, but he was also the new driver of Old Bess, the grand old steam locomotive Sam had been in love with since the age of six. And probably before, judging by the photo

Uncle Ken had shown him of his dad holding Sam in front of her as a baby. Love of railway engines ran in the family.

Much as he loved Bess, her place in his heart as the most beautiful thing in the universe had been finally, unexpectedly, challenged. Ryan Saunders was perfect. The only flaw he possessed was a small scar by the corner of his left eye, and it almost seemed as if that imperfection was there to demonstrate the flawlessness of the rest of him. He had short, stylish dark-blond hair that was a world away from the tangled mess of Sam's brown mop and a strong jawline that was often dusted with light stubble, just enough to make him look slightly dangerous and to have Sam wonder how it would feel rubbing over his skin. His lips were full, with a small indentation in the lower one that had Sam's brain working overtime about how those generous, soft-looking lips would feel against his.

He tore his gaze away from the figure on the platform. It would be easier later when Ryan wasn't strutting around in jeans that fitted him like a glove—if that glove happened to be made of old, faded denim that wrapped tightly around the curve of his arse, the muscle of his thigh, and cupped snugly around a very intriguing bump behind the zip of his flies. It would be easier because Ryan would be in baggy overalls, and he'd look through Sam the way he always did, the way most people did. And then Sam would be able to concentrate on the trains and think about how beautiful Bess looked in the sunshine and how that was enough for him.

She was enough for him. She'd have to be. She was all he'd ever have.

He turned and trudged across the bridge. Somehow his joy in the morning had gone.

RYAN

Ryan was early for work. He hadn't exactly had a lot of jobs in his life, but he'd never turned up early to any of them before this one. It was somehow becoming a common occurrence these days, probably because this didn't feel like a job. He got to drive a beautiful old steam locomotive, safely removed from the sticky-fingered kids who clambered around the carriages she drew and the nerdy trainspotter types who wanted to know what her nominal tractive effort was, and all he had to worry about was the open track in front of him and taking care of his girl, Bessie.

Bessie, or *Elizabeth of Shrewsbury* to give her the honour of her official name, was a beauty. He wasn't the only one to think that way, because every summer she was rolled out as a tourist attraction and every summer her carriages filled with anyone who had enough money for a ticket and who wanted to remember what train travel should be about. It was about puffing through the countryside behind a classic piece of engineering, not overcrowded carriages where nearly everyone was on their phone or playing music so loudly he didn't understand why they bothered with earbuds.

Not that Ryan hated his fellow men. Especially not on a Saturday night, when the clubs were buzzing. Right then he *loved* his fellow men. Frequently, and usually in the bathroom. Or at least he *had*, right up until he found out about the random drug and alcohol checks this job entailed. These days he was practically trapped in this dead-end town, where the only saving grace was Bessie.

Dead-end town or not, today was likely to be busy if the promised temperatures materialised. Glancing up at the clear blue sky, he saw a figure on the bridge above the track. Who the hell else would be about this early? He'd left Simon building the fire in Bessie's belly in his usual silent, concentrated way. There weren't any trains due for another hour.

And then he saw the hunched shoulders in the shapeless hoodie and vaguely recognised him as the guy who always hung around the place midweek. He never took a ride on Bessie, but he couldn't tear his eyes from her as she came majestically into the station and stopped at the platform, occasionally emitting hisses of steam as Ryan blew off the cylinder cocks to let condensation escape. The way everyone jumped at the noise was just a bonus.

Ryan was wandering along the platform, heading for the staffroom and a cup of tea, just as Hoodie Guy came down off the bridge.

"Morning," Ryan murmured, because it was too rude even for him to ignore the guy when they were the only two people around for five miles or so.

"Hello," the guy said, glancing at him then away. His cheeks turned bright pink as he clutched his satchel closely in front of him.

A fricking *satchel*? Ryan didn't think he'd ever seen one in real life before, just in old films and stuff. But that cleared up who this guy was—one of the nerdy trainspotters who Bessie attracted.

"You're driving Bess today?" Hoodie Guy's words came out so twisted up and stumbling over one another it took Ryan a moment to disentangle them enough to understand what he'd asked. By that point the hopeful look in the guy's face had disappeared and Ryan had seen happier-looking kicked puppies.

"Yeah," he said, and it took every bit of strength he had not to ask why the hell else would he be standing on a station platform at six o'clock in the morning. "Simon's getting her ready."

"She's beautiful," the kid said, and he was smiling suddenly, all self-consciousness gone. If Ryan had seen that face at a club, he'd have been interested, with those dimples in his cheeks and dark eyes shining. But he wasn't. Because the kid was, in case Ryan had managed to forget, clutching a fricking *satchel*.

"Yeah," he said again, and with a slight nod, moved on.

Because, jeez, any minute now the kid was going to be asking about fusible plugs and brake cylinder psi and all the other stuff that the wannabe engine drivers wanted to know. He didn't know whether that level of interest was better or worse than the people who thought being an engine driver meant he just stood on the footplate watching the world go by.

On the plus side, mentioning what he did for a living was a pretty good guarantee of getting laid. It turned out a whole lot of guys had some sort of fantasy about muscular, shirtless guys stoking the fire of an engine. It was a fantasy he might have shared if not for the fact that Simon, his fireman, never took his shirt off, and thank God for that, because he was the furthest thing from sexy that Ryan could imagine.

But even though Simon was the least sexy thing Ryan had encountered since he'd had his balls waxed—once. Only once. He would *never* do that again—the man knew his job. He knew what size of coal lumps Bessie liked best and exactly where to place them to keep her running like a dream. He didn't say a word that wasn't necessary, and Ryan couldn't ask for a better fellow traveller. Unless he'd been sexy and shirtless, of course. Because Ryan might concentrate hard when he drove Bessie, but he was only human. He wouldn't have minded a bit of eye candy while he worked.

He opened the door to the staffroom and glanced back to find Hoodie Guy sitting on what Ryan now realised was his usual bench, satchel clutched to his chest as he looked down the track away from Ryan. Something about the way he was sitting there on his own, with no train due for another hour, tugged at Ryan's heart.

But then he remembered the satchel, which probably held a high-spec video camera for filming trains, along with spreadsheets of engine serial numbers, and he came back to his senses. He'd have a cup of tea, climb into his overalls and get Bessie rolling.

SAM

Sam didn't relax until he heard the door closing behind Ryan Saunders. And then he finally let go of his death grip on his satchel and put it on the bench beside him.

God, what had he been *thinking*, trying to talk to Ryan Saunders? There was just something about the way Ryan had looked at him, had *seen* him for the first time and said hello, with his eyes crinkling at the corners in a smile, that had made something inside Sam flutter with excitement. He now realised that Ryan hadn't been smiling at him but had merely been screwing his eyes up slightly against the sun. He'd just been being polite, made obvious by the way he'd so quickly moved on when Sam had tried to say something else.

He opened his satchel and pulled his notebook out. He knew even other railway enthusiasts laughed at him for doing it the old-fashioned way, but it was the way his dad had taught him, the way *his* father had taught *him*, and it made him feel closer to his dad every time he got out his old exercise book and pencil to write down engine numbers.

It wasn't like he was living in the Stone Age for everything. If not for the Internet, he wouldn't have what passed for a social life, let alone a sex life. Once he'd discovered the rail enthusiasts' message boards as a twelve-year-old, and worked out some years later how to disable the adult filter Uncle Ken had put on his laptop and found porn sites, his life had improved immeasurably. And these days he had a phone, so he could watch porn more comfortably when lying in bed. He *loved* technology. Just not for this. This had to be done properly.

Twelve hours later, Sam was packing up his satchel again. The last of the daytrippers had gone, flowing up the platform and across the bridge like a sunburned river, chattering excitedly about riding behind "a real steam engine". The thing Sam had never been able to understand was precisely why that was so exciting, because they were sitting *behind* Bess. From inside the carriages, they couldn't possibly see her and appreciate the grace in the synchronous movement of her pistons or the way her brass dome glinted in the sunlight.

Having disgorged her passengers, she'd set off back to her shed for the night. There were still some more trains to come through this evening, but Sam felt he'd had enough. He'd run out of tea a few hours ago and he was getting hungry. The shadows were lengthening slightly, though it was still warm enough for him not to have put his hoodie back on. It was good to feel the sun on his skin after what had so far been a damp, cold spring.

He was rolling his hoodie up to tuck it under his arm when he became aware of footsteps along the platform and glanced up, because he'd thought he was alone. Ryan Saunders was approaching from the direction of Bess's shed.

Unlike this morning, when he'd reminded Sam of a big cat sauntering through its territory, he looked a little weary. There was a soot mark on his cheek and he'd undone the top half of his dark blue overalls, pushing them down off his torso and tying the sleeves at the waist to reveal strong arms and a faded black T-shirt stretched across a broad, muscular chest.

As Sam's eyes travelled over the figure walking towards him, he found the way the sleeves were tied drew his gaze to Ryan's crotch. He wondered how easily those overalls would fall all the way down. They'd need only a tiny bit of help, he was sure, and would reveal tight, faded jeans that would be so easy just to unzip and… He suddenly realised he was staring and jerked his gaze back up guiltily.

To his horror, Ryan had caught him looking. "You're not going to find a serial number on *that*," he said, and the amusement in his voice meant Sam could breathe again. It seemed as if Ryan wasn't going to beat him up. There was never any excuse for looking at another guy's dick uninvited. He'd learned that lesson early and learned it well.

"I just—" he said, getting to his feet and clutching his satchel across his chest, his cheeks heating.

And then he stood there tongue-tied, because what the hell was he supposed to say? *I think you're really hot and I was wondering what it would be like to touch you?* It might be true, but he didn't think he could ever say it to anyone. Certainly not to Ryan Saunders, who had heads turning wherever he went.

Ryan smirked. "It's the price I pay for being irresistible."

That egotistical remark should have made him completely resistible, then and there. But somehow it didn't. His gaze was running over Sam, until Sam had to fight the urge to cross his arms defensively. He knew this T-shirt was a little tight. He probably should have thrown it away after he'd started working out and put on some muscle for the first time in his life, but he could practically hear Uncle Ken's voice in his ear telling him there was still plenty of wear in it. And it wasn't like anyone ever looked at him anyway.

Except, apparently, Ryan Saunders, whose eyebrows were slightly raised as he studied him.

"You're kind of built for a nerd, aren't you?" he said. "I guess trainspotting's a more active hobby than I'd thought."

Sam should have walked away because this guy was *insufferable*. Except there was humour gleaming in those eyes as well as something else. Something that if he wasn't entirely losing his mind was actual, sexual interest.

In *him,* Sam Chancellor.

"It's all that running alongside the engines to get the numbers down," he blurted out before he could stop himself.

To his amazement, Ryan laughed. A true laugh that caused his eyes to crinkle at the corners. It made him even more gorgeous than he already was.

"Ryan Saunders," he said. "I drive old Bessie."

"Bessie?" Sam was horrified at the heresy. "She's *Bess*. She's *always* been Bess."

"Given I'm the one whose hands have been over every inch of her, I guess she's allowing me intimacies the general public doesn't get," Ryan said.

The low seductive voice and the thought of Ryan's hands stroking over him the way they did over Bess meant Sam was getting hard. He clutched his satchel in front of him like some sort of shield, except that wasn't helping at all because it was pressed against his dick and, God above, he was about to get a hard-on, here and now, right in front of Ryan Saunders.

"You haven't told me your name," Ryan said.

"Sam," he choked out. "Sam Chancellor, and I have to go."

He put his head down and fled.

RYAN

Well, that was interesting. Sam Chancellor had most definitely been checking him out. He'd also gone from looking like a gangly fifteen-year-old huddled in a shapeless grey hoodie to something else entirely, stretched out unselfconsciously on the bench in a way that showed off his long legs and surprisingly broad shoulders. Not to mention some of the most enticingly muscled arms Ryan had seen in a while.

Stripped of his hoodie and his self-consciousness, he wasn't gangly and he most definitely wasn't fifteen years old. Closer to twenty-five would be Ryan's guess. His hair was a shaggy mess, but the way his dark eyes sparkled and his cheeks dimpled when he smiled somehow made the whole hair thing look endearing rather than the disaster zone it actually was.

And, to repeat, he'd *definitely* been checking Ryan out. Ryan was used to being checked out and he knew it when he saw it. So why Sam had scuttled off as if the hounds of hell were on his heels just as things were getting interesting, Ryan had no idea.

Damn it. It left him with an itch he wanted to scratch and no way of doing so. It wasn't only the prospect of blood tests that stopped him clubbing these days; it was the knowledge that he needed to be alert the whole time he was driving Bessie. If he gave in to temptation and went to a club in the city, he wouldn't stop at just one drink—he'd party till four in the morning, and he was due here at six.

And the truth was, he preferred driving Bessie to some frantic coupling in the backroom of some club. Not that he had any intention of swearing off sex in order to drive a train, but now he was heading towards thirty, some things were becoming just a bit stale.

His lips twisted as he let himself into the staffroom and climbed out of his overalls. If anyone ever heard him say such a thing, he'd probably have to kill them. Casual was Ryan's middle name. He loved brief hookups. He didn't want anything else and it wasn't as if he'd ever been short of offers. He knew he looked good and he knew how to use it. But not when it came to Sam Chancellor, apparently.

Frowning, he stashed his overalls in the locker and shrugged on his battered leather jacket. He guessed the kid was too much of a nerd—*oh*. If he was really that much of a trainspotter, the kid was probably a virgin. It wasn't that Ryan was losing his touch.

Well, that was something of a relief. It didn't stop him banging the staffroom door behind him with more force than necessary, because although he'd solved the puzzle of why Sam had fled, he was still left with the stirrings of interest deep in his stomach and no way of working them out except for his right hand. And come *on*, he shouldn't have to resort to that.

He ran lightly up the steps of the footbridge, then paused at the top, looking along the tracks that led into the gently rolling hills surrounding the town. He loved that view when there was no one else here, just him and Bessie. And then he caught himself—he didn't love anything about this town. It was just another place to stay a while.

He was frowning as he strode out of the station, but stopped short, unhappiness forgotten in his enjoyment of the unexpected sight that met his eyes. Sam Chancellor was being lectured by an old woman who was about two-thirds his height. She was reaching up to shake her finger in his face. And instead of moving away from her like any sane person would, Sam was hunched and pink-cheeked, looking like a puppy who'd been caught peeing on the carpet.

Ryan quickened his pace so he could find out what was happening. Maybe he could swoop in and rescue the kid, who'd be so grateful he'd spread his legs and beg Ryan to fuck him.

Yeah, like *that* was going to happen. But he kept going anyway, just in case.

Chapter Two

RYAN

"And don't you think to do that again! You hear me, young man?"

Ryan bit his lip, *hard*, to stop himself smirking at the look on Sam's face when he saw Ryan approaching. His evident hope that this might be an escape was mixed with mortification that Ryan had witnessed the scolding he was enduring.

"No, Mrs Verity," he said. "I'm sorry."

She patted his arm. "You're a good boy, Sam."

She strode off, her carriage fiercely upright and her wavy white hair looking as if it was glued into position. Or perhaps it daren't move because it was as terrified of her as Sam so obviously was.

"You get caught scrumping apples from her garden?" Ryan asked, wandering over to where Sam was clinging onto that freakish satchel of his again and squirming with embarrassment.

He shook his head. "I mowed her lawn for her," he confessed, his cheeks pink.

"Well, no wonder she was pissed off. What the hell were you *thinking*, doing something nice like that for someone?"

Sam's lips quirked. "Apparently she thinks I should be spending my time—" He broke off and his cheeks blazed. "Anyway," he said, gripping the strap of his satchel and looking as if he was about to make a run for it again.

"You doing anything now?" Ryan asked.

Sam's mouth fell open in astonishment and he gaped at Ryan, obviously not knowing what to say.

Ryan realised he'd need to lay it out more bluntly. "I could do with a pint after a long day, and maybe blow off a little steam afterwards. Thought you might be interested."

"I—uh, well—did you just say 'blow off steam'?" Sam asked. "*Really?*"

And when he wasn't stuttering and self-conscious, he was *fun*. None of the twinks who'd sucked him off had ever questioned Ryan's corny line. In fact, half of them had made what they thought were original and hilarious jokes about coupling and shunting.

"At least I didn't ask if you wanted to blow my cylinder cock," Ryan said, and the colour that had been fading in Sam's cheeks flared hotter and brighter than Bessie's fire.

"Ah, Saunders. Just the person I wanted to see."

Ryan tore his gaze from Sam's face. "Mr Cleaver," he said, fighting the temptation to smack his head into the nearest wall in frustration. He hated the guy anyway, but this timing could *not* be worse.

"Walk with me," Cleaver said, already setting off in the direction of his BMW parked by the kerb—on double-yellow lines, of course—as if he knew Ryan would obediently follow.

Ryan shrugged helplessly at Sam. *My boss*, he mouthed. By the time he caught up with Cleaver, Sam's forlorn-looking figure was disappearing up the street.

Well, okay, maybe it wasn't looking forlorn but instead surprisingly buff for a trainspotter. It was Ryan's dick that was feeling forlorn because he had been well and truly cock-blocked.

It was only when Cleaver's eyes rested on his face and he saw the expression in them that he realised that might be the least of his worries.

SAM

Sam was left staring like an idiot as Ryan followed the guy in a suit towards a shiny silver car. Because had Ryan Saunders just...? He must have got it wrong. No way had Ryan Saunders just suggested he and *Sam*...

And then he realised his gaze was glued to that perfect arse in those tight faded jeans and that he was standing in the middle of the pavement where anyone might see him staring at another guy's arse.

He turned abruptly on his heel and headed for home. He wasn't an idiot. He might not be comfortable around people, but he wasn't an *idiot*. And Ryan Saunders had definitely been cracking on to him.

Blowing off steam. He snorted, suddenly thankful that Ryan Saunders wasn't completely perfect after all. Not if he thought a line like *that* would get him into Sam's jeans. Although it wasn't as if his getting into them was exactly a challenge, because Sam knew that Ryan Saunders was *way* out of his league and he'd grab the opportunity with both very eager hands. Ryan might have been poking fun at Sam for being a nerd, but it hadn't been in a *mean* way, the way Sam was used to. But then that guy, his boss, had turned up, and that was that.

It was just as well, otherwise Ryan Saunders would have realised what he was doing and backed off. He'd either have laughed at Sam for thinking he'd meant it or suddenly remembered he had somewhere else to be, even though he'd been kind enough not to snigger too much at Sam getting ticked off by Mrs Verity.

Her blood had been up as she made her way to the Local History Society meeting to do battle with the history teacher from the high school who didn't have a clue what he was talking about, apparently. And then she'd spotted Sam and taken him to task. It had been a warm-up for the history teacher, Sam thought, feeling sorry for the hapless man who'd dared incur her displeasure.

Mrs Verity was eighty-seven years old, but neither her mind nor her will had faltered in the least. It was just her body that was beginning to let her down, which was why he'd been mowing her lawn for her the past three years, taking over when Uncle Ken had no longer been well enough to do it. And then a month ago she'd told him she was paying a gardener to come in and that he wasn't needed any more. Which had been fine, until he'd passed her house on the way back from work and noticed the lawn was getting long and looking neglected, so he'd popped back and done it for her. It was only now that she'd told him the real reason he'd been replaced—she thought he was spending too much of his time with the old folk in the town, his uncle's friends, and should be making friends of his own.

"And meeting someone special," she'd added. He still didn't know if she realised he was gay, but from the way she never said "a nice girl", he thought she probably did.

He sighed as he gave his front door the shove it needed to open. She had a point. Sometimes it felt as if he'd slipped into Uncle Ken's life when he'd died. But it wasn't as if Sam had any friends of his own except for the people he talked to online about trains, and he wasn't going to make any at work, because his colleagues were all women who seemed to think he needed mothering. Maybe he should do something different, but he didn't know what.

And the problem wasn't the town—it was *him*. If he did sell the house and move away, he'd end up living somewhere on his own where he didn't know anyone. At least here he had Uncle Ken's friends, and one or two of the people he'd gone to school with occasionally said hi to him if they passed in the street. Once out of school, the tribal urge to destroy the weakest in the class dissipated, or so it seemed—he hadn't been beaten up for almost eight years.

He made his way through the sitting room to the kitchen, flicked the kettle on for a cup of tea and opened the fridge, where the other half of the chicken casserole he'd made the previous night sat on the shelf waiting for him to take it out and warm it through. Something in him rebelled. It was what he did every single Tuesday night, eating chicken casserole in front of the TV before getting online and talking about the trains he'd seen that day, then taking a shower and ending up in bed looking at other sorts of websites.

But today wasn't like any other day. Today—and he still couldn't quite believe he'd got this right—Ryan Saunders had been interested in him.

The sound of the doorbell made him realise he was staring blankly at the casserole and letting all the cold air escape. He closed the fridge and went to see who was at the door.

"I brought you some asparagus, dear," Mrs Goodall said, pushing a plastic container at him which was filled to the brim with asparagus spears. "I know you don't have any in your garden, and

Leslie's growing his own this year, so I've got more than I know what to do with."

"Thank you." Sam mumbled it because he didn't really like asparagus, but he could never tell her that. Not that she'd ever ask. "Would you like to come in?"

"Just for a minute," she said. "I won't stay. I'm on my way to Stella's supper party."

That fact didn't stop her following him into the kitchen and talking nonstop as he tipped the asparagus out onto the counter and started washing the plastic container to give back to her. Anything to stop her dropping by again later to pick it up.

In the early days after Uncle Ken's death, he'd been deeply thankful to see a friendly face at the door whenever one of his uncle's Garden Club friends had called in with a box of fruit or vegetables. It had eased his desperate loneliness. But when the sharp ache of loss finally began to ease, he found their visits more depressing than anything else. They'd pop in "just for a minute", smiles on their faces as they spoke about what they'd been doing lately, rubbing it in that every old-age pensioner in Cardale had more of a social life than he did. They talked *at* him rather than *to* him, and on the rare occasion they asked him a question about his life, it was usually whether he had potato blight in his garden.

Mrs Verity wasn't like that. Her sharp mind and sharper tongue terrified Sam, but she *saw* him, whereas the rest of them made him think that "Keep an eye on Ken's nephew whatshisname" had been one of the motions passed at the Garden Club AGM. They were kind and probably did care about him in their own way, but they weren't people he could *talk* to, not like he'd been able to do with Uncle Ken. And so he buried himself in the railway forums that Val thought were so hilarious and found company and friendship that way, and tried not to care that it was all through a screen.

He tuned in again to Mrs Goodall, who was involved in some long story about how she'd left her credit card at the supermarket and hadn't noticed until she'd got home. He nodded and smiled in the right places, desperately fighting back the loneliness that threatened to swallow him.

RYAN

"So you see my problem, Ryan," Cleaver said. He'd driven them to the centre of town, where he'd led the way into the old coaching inn tucked into a corner of the market square.

"I don't see how I can help you," Ryan said over his orange juice. He'd figured he should steer clear of alcohol in front of the boss, even though he wasn't due to drive Bessie for another fourteen hours.

Frustration flared in Cleaver's eyes. Ryan couldn't blame him. The man had hinted so broadly it was bloody obvious what he wanted. But if this old bastard wanted him to do it, he should have the guts to damn well ask outright.

"I merely thought, with your father's position and his interest in the railway here, he might see his way to helping us through this rough patch," he said. "Once the summer's here and the visitor numbers increase, there won't be any problem, but with the extra work the engine needed over the winter, we're—well, I'm sorry to say we're in a spot of bother, Ryan."

A spot of bother which he thought could be solved by Ryan crawling to his father to ask for more money to add to the sizeable donation he'd made just after Ryan had been employed as Bessie's driver.

Ryan stared at Cleaver, keeping his face carefully blank despite the turmoil inside him. "No," he said flatly. "If you want more money, you ask him. It's nothing to do with me."

"But you see, Ryan, a man like your father must have so many requests for financial aid, and you could explain it to him the way no one else—"

"I said *no*." He was on his feet, trembling slightly before he caught himself and shoved his hands in the pockets of his jeans, desperate not to show anything to the bastard in front of him. "If that's all," he got out between gritted teeth.

Cleaver leaned back on the plush velvet bench and spread his arms along the top of it. He was doing the same thing Ryan's father always did—using body language to underline his dominance. Ryan was standing with his hands shoved in the front pocket of his jeans, making his shoulders hunched. But he couldn't stand any other way because he had to hold himself together. Today had been such a good day, and then this had come out of nowhere. It had blindsided him.

"The thing is, Ryan, if we don't get some sizeable donations from somewhere soon, I'm going to have to start laying people off. And I'd hate to lose you."

The threat wasn't exactly a surprise, because that was the kind of man Cleaver was. It still felt like a kick in the gut. He knew he hadn't got this job on merit—however good he was, he didn't have the amount of experience so many other guys did—but he'd wanted it so badly he'd swallowed all of his pride, dignity and self-esteem and asked his father for a favour. And it had all been for nothing because he was going to be fired.

"I can't help you," he said, and turned and walked out.

SAM

Sam stood under the warm spray of the shower, his eyes closed as the water cascaded over him. It felt good, clinging to every part of his body, the sting of the high pressure bringing his nerve endings alive through the slight buzz he had going from the beer he'd had with his supper.

After finally seeing Mrs Goodall on her way, he'd gone to the off-licence and bought some beer, and then to the chippy and got fish and chips. He'd eaten them in front of the TV and hadn't felt the least bit guilty about the healthy chicken casserole and asparagus sitting in his fridge. Instead he'd felt triumphant, as if he'd kicked over some traces he hadn't known existed.

When he'd finished his supper, he'd reached for his laptop and looked at the login screen for his favourite train forum. After a while, he'd closed the lid and put the laptop down on the couch beside him. Because today there'd been Bess and there'd been the 3.06 that had the HST power cars, but neither of those things held the same interest as usual. He wanted to think instead of how it had felt when Ryan Saunders had looked at him, eyes assessing and interested. And the way Ryan looked when he walked, the way his jeans clung so softly and tightly to his leanly muscled thighs and the loving way they skimmed the curve of his arse. He'd swallowed, his mouth getting dry, and because he was *not* going to sit and wank on the couch, he'd gone to take a shower.

Now he was safely under the spray of water and thinking again about Ryan, his stomach was tight and heavy with want. If that stupid man hadn't come over to take Ryan away, Sam could have had his hands on the most perfect arse in the history of the world right now, feeling that warm skin over firm muscle for himself. His cock was filling at the very thought of it. At how he might, even now, be clutching at that arse as Ryan slid inside him.

His hand felt good, wrapping around his cock as he worked himself, but not as good as it would feel to have Ryan deep inside him, hard and thick and hot, and fucking him with all the muscle in that perfect body, pushing in hard and fast, until all Sam could do would be to take it, again and again, so big, filling him. He whimpered as he came, spurting into the curtain of falling water, his knees weak.

He turned off the shower and got out, wiping a slightly unsteady hand across the condensation that had gathered on the mirror so he could look at himself. His hair was a mess, plastered to his head, but there wasn't much he could do about that. His hair did what it would, regardless of the hairdresser's best efforts.

His eyes looked back at him and there was a new determination burning in them. Mrs Verity had been right, even if it was disturbing to think of her when he was standing here naked. He could live the rest of his life the way he'd lived the last two years, since Uncle Ken had died, or he could *do* something.

The mirror was clouding again, but as he turned away to snag a towel from the rail, things had never looked clearer to him. Tomorrow he would go to the station and he would let Ryan Saunders know just how interested he was. And if Ryan had thought better of it, or had found someone else, well, Sam was still going to do *something*. He didn't know what, but he was twenty-four years old and living like he was seventy. That ended now.

Chapter Three

RYAN

The alarm blared, jolting Ryan awake. Fucking typical. He'd only got to sleep an hour ago and suddenly it was time to get up.

He was still half-asleep when he stumbled into the wet room and fumbled with the shower, hissing when it came through too cold. At least it woke him up, and by the time he'd had a mug of coffee and a cursory shave, and got dressed, he was feeling more alert. But there was still that heavy, sick feeling in his stomach, the one that had stopped him sleeping.

He wasn't going to do what Cleaver wanted. That meant he wouldn't be able to drive Bessie for much longer, and it was the first thing he'd enjoyed since he couldn't remember when. Driving a steam train had been nothing more than a barely remembered childhood dream when he'd followed a wild impulse to sign up for a training course.

In his saner moments he'd wondered what the hell he was doing. But he'd ended up loving every minute of the exhaustive training. He'd finally found something that posed mental and physical challenges. He'd had to work hard. He'd had to *think*. It had satisfied him the way nothing else had. He'd hated maths and physics at school—he'd hated *school* for that matter, with all those rules, and teachers telling him what to do and how to do it—but finding an actual use for all that stuff had been like a light coming on. Not to mention that the very first time he'd got to drive an engine himself had been almost as good as sex.

Well, maybe not quite that good, he decided, adjusting himself in his jeans because it had been several weeks since he'd last fucked anyone and his deprived cock had reacted at the very thought of sex. But it was still better than anything calling itself a job deserved to be. And now he was going to be out on his ear and moving on again, to God only knew where and what.

He let the front door to the building slam shut behind him, even though he knew it pissed off everyone else who lived in the flats to be woken at dawn. It wasn't like he'd be sticking around to hear the complaints anyway. Swinging his leg over his bike, he started her up, revving the engine with an ear-splitting roar just to make sure that anyone who'd slept through the slammed door was now fully awake. And then he pulled out onto the empty street and headed for the station.

SAM

Sam found himself humming in the shower as he washed with extra care. He had to be perfect today. It all seemed so easy, right up until he went into his room to get dressed.

Thirty minutes later, he had a pile of clothes on his bed and his stomach was twisting with frustration and fear as he tried to decide what on earth he should wear. He was going to miss the London express if he didn't make a decision soon. But all his clothes were chosen for comfort and it always felt safer to wear them slightly baggy so he wouldn't attract attention. That was fine, except that for the first time he *wanted* to get someone's attention.

Sod it. He could stay here paralysed with indecision the rest of the day and not even see Ryan, or he could just wear what he'd worn yesterday because that hadn't stopped Ryan flirting with him. He pulled on the same pair of jeans and another of those slightly too-tight T-shirts, and headed for the door.

Once out of the house, he realised what a stupid decision that had been because it was too cold to be out without a hoodie. His nipples were hard, protesting points against his T-shirt, and as soon as he became aware of that, he wondered if Ryan would notice too. Maybe he'd sneer at Sam for being too dumb to dress for the weather, or maybe he'd want to find out for himself what else might make his nipples tight and hard. And if he kept thinking that way, Sam was going to have a hard-on before he even *saw* Ryan Saunders.

He gripped his satchel tightly and thought about the 9.47 from Hereford. He didn't know what was going on at the depot there, but for the last three Wednesdays it had been in reverse formation, and he wasn't the only one to have noticed. Current bets on the forum ranged from the staff at the depot being a bunch of dopeheads to them doing it just to screw with people. By the time he reached the station, he was relaxed again and looking forward to seeing the outrageous theories some of the funnier forum members came up with this evening to explain it. It wouldn't be Sam—he wasn't any good at making people laugh—but he enjoyed reading what they had to say.

"Hey, Sam."

He jumped. He'd been miles away and Val had caught him. "Hi," he said, and pretended it didn't come out sounding like a squeak. "I better go—I need to catch—"

"You missed the express," she said. He hadn't realised she was as aware of the trains as he was. Then again, she'd worked here since leaving school six years ago, so he guessed it made sense. "Are you okay? You *never* miss the express."

And suddenly, instead of sounding nosy, or interfering, or intimidating, she sounded like she was worried about him. He darted a glance at her face and there was concern in the blue eyes beneath the eyebrow piercing.

"I got distracted," he confessed, glancing down involuntarily at his jeans. For an insane moment, he thought about asking her where most people bought their clothes because he knew it wasn't where he did—the same shop Uncle Ken had always used and had taken him to as a kid, though in Sam's defence, it made sense for him to keep buying his stuff from there because these days he got a staff discount. He'd love to know how Ryan Saunders's jeans looked like they were made for him and Sam's looked like they were destined for someone at least three sizes bigger and who was a completely different shape.

Reality asserted itself. The last thing he needed was to get caught up in some sort of "straight eye for the queer guy" scenario, because he had the sinking feeling she wouldn't just tell him where to shop but would actually take him shopping and make him try on everything before telling him what he should buy. She never wore the same outfit twice so far as he could see, her hair was a different colour every week, and frankly she terrified him, with her confidence and the fact she really seemed not to give a damn what anyone thought of her. He smiled nervously at her and edged away.

"I better..." he said, and thank God she nodded and he could get out of there.

He paused in the middle of the footbridge on the way to Bess's platform, the one that was away from all the others as she ran on a specially restored loop of railway around the valley, keeping off the main lines that the modern trains used. He knew there were no trains due, but this way it would seem as if he were checking for any, while really he was scouring the platform looking for Ryan. The excitement that had been bubbling up inside him slowly faded as he realised there was no sign of that sexy figure prowling along Platform 5 the way he usually did at this time in the morning, heading for the staffroom once he'd got the first preparations on Bess done.

Deflated, he clutched his satchel tightly to him. It had never occurred to him that Ryan might not be there. Just as his stomach hollowed with disappointment, he saw Ryan at the far end of the platform, sauntering casually in his direction. His mouth dry and his underarms feeling suddenly sweaty, Sam forced himself to continue across the bridge and down the steps.

Reaching the platform, his breath caught as he took in all over again the way Ryan moved, his easy stride full of predatory grace. But as Ryan got close to where he was standing rooted to the spot, clutching his satchel to him, Sam could see lines of strain in his face that hadn't been there yesterday. Lines that made him look less like a sex god and more like a tired human being, one whose eyes were dark with some sort of emotion.

"Hey," Sam said breathlessly as Ryan would have walked straight past. He was damn well keeping his resolution not to let life pass him by any longer.

Ryan jerked his head round, but it took him a while to see Sam. Or to recognise him. Sam's stomach turned over.

"Hi," he said at last, but it seemed like he was miles away.

"Sorry, didn't meant to interrupt," Sam gabbled, backing off, because God, he was an idiot. A complete and utter idiot for even thinking that a few words between them one afternoon, words which Ryan would have forgotten about already, could have meant anything.

"Yeah, no," Ryan said, then shook his head. "Sorry," he said. "I need coffee. Didn't get much sleep."

As he spoke, his gaze was running over Sam. Sam went against every instinct he possessed and let go of his satchel from where he was huddling protectively behind it, allowing it to hang down by his side. Imperceptibly, he hoped, he straightened his shoulders. And bingo—Ryan's eyes were drawn to where his nipples were still announcing their displeasure at the air temperature.

"Maybe I'll see you later?" Sam said, hugely daring, and was rewarded with a smirk.

"Sure as hell hope so," Ryan said, before turning to push open the blue-painted door marked *Staff Only*. "Catch you later, Sam," he said, and it was all Sam could do not to cartwheel down the platform. If that wasn't a promise, he didn't know what was. And Ryan had remembered his name.

He finally managed to control the grin that was making his cheeks ache and shuffled along the platform to where he could sit down on a bench and pull out his notebook, readying it for today's trains. Life just didn't get any better than this.

RYAN

Ryan climbed down from Bessie, giving her a fond slap as he did so. He was tired and stiff, but it wasn't her fault. It was the end result of a long day in which he'd been rigid as he'd guided her around the familiar ten mile loop of line, blowing the whistle every now and then at the kids—and adults—who stopped to wave excitedly as she passed by. All his usual joy in her had gone because he knew this wasn't going to last.

He guessed he'd known it all along. Nothing good ever lasted. Most of the time that was his fault, but not this time. This time he'd done everything right, had worked his arse off to be the best driver he could be because she deserved it and more. But despite everything he'd done, he'd seen a familiar sort of greed in Cleaver's eyes when he'd spoken to Ryan yesterday. Even in the middle of the night, when Ryan had wondered in a moment of madness if he *could* go back to his father, cap in hand, he'd known it wouldn't solve anything. A man like Cleaver wouldn't let it go at just one bailout. He'd keep coming back for more.

No, he had to be ready to move on, and maybe he'd find something else he loved as much as he loved this. And maybe there was a pig or two up there floating around.

He forced himself to concentrate on helping Simon clean Bessie's ash pan. There was a whole lot of maintenance that needed doing on a daily basis to keep her running safely, though they did the bulk of it when she was closed to the public on a Thursday. On those days they were joined by a qualified engineer and by Ritchie and Amit, who spent the rest of the week selling tickets, shepherding passengers and acting as train dispatchers. At the end of a Thursday, with her every need tended to and polished until her brass sparkled, Bessie looked like a queen rather than the old workhorse she'd once been.

Finally they were done. While Ryan was locking Bessie's shed, Simon headed off home to do whatever he did when he wasn't stoking Bessie's boiler fire. Ryan seemed to remember he kept bees, but he'd never been interested enough to ask for details.

When Ryan reached the platform, Simon was climbing the bridge, his steps slower than they'd been that morning. Ryan thought that a day of shovelling coal would do that to a man. Thankfully, though he'd had to master the technique and learn when and how much to load, he'd never done much of that himself. He'd been able to concentrate on the fun part. The part which he'd probably never have again.

Bleakness swept through him, but as he stared up the empty platform, his gaze was met by a pair of bright, inquisitive eyes. That Sam guy was still there, sitting on his bench, that damn satchel by his side, and he was smiling at Ryan. Excited and hopeful, and the light in those eyes was more than Ryan could resist even in his gloom.

His lips twisted in an attempt at a smile as he started over to where Sam was sitting with his long legs stretched out in front of him and his arms crossed over his chest. Which was a shame, because from what Ryan could see, that was a very nice chest indeed. But the arms were tempting too—shaped with muscle without being too bulky.

Ryan's evening was suddenly looking up. He thrust away all thoughts of any future beyond the next two hours, and this time his smile was genuine.

SAM

It had been the longest day Sam had ever known, torn as he was between anticipation about talking to Ryan and terror about talking to Ryan. When Ryan had left the staffroom earlier that morning, wearing his baggy dark blue overalls, he'd nodded at Sam, who'd been sitting on his usual bench and trying not to shiver in the low sun. As Sam had watched him walking away down the platform, his mouth had dried because even in those overalls, the perfection of that arse could not be ignored. He wanted to get close to Ryan Saunders as much as he'd wanted anything in his whole life.

Although he enjoyed noting numbers, moving between platforms because he knew the timetables off by heart and the best vantage points to view each train coming in—and today's Hereford train looked like it had been put together by a four-year-old and he couldn't wait to get onto the forum and find out what everyone else made of that—it didn't leave him with the usual feeling of satisfaction. Not when the rest of him was waiting, heart pounding every time he thought of it, for the evening. For when Ryan Saunders would saunter back up from that engine shed and stop in front of him, his eyes crinkled around the corners in a smile as he slid the zip of his overalls down in open invitation.

He jerked out of his imaginings when he saw the real thing heading towards him and got to his feet nervously, hands suddenly sweaty. God. Ryan Saunders was looking at him. He was *seeing* him. Sam swallowed convulsively, torn between dread and excitement.

RYAN

Jeez, the kid was tall. Ryan had forgotten that. He'd also forgotten just how long those legs were. He couldn't wait to have those hellishly unflattering jeans off him and to sink into the tightness of his arse. He needed this. It had been too long.

"Saunders. A moment, if you please."

And he was either going to weep and bang his head against the closest surface, or punch Cleaver in his smug-looking face. What *was* it with this guy? Did he have a master's in cock-blocking or something?

"What?" It came out as a snarl as he pivoted on his heel to see Cleaver closing the distance between them. The man was still breathing heavily from having navigated the footbridge with all its steps, and Ryan wondered what could be so urgent that he hadn't just waited on the other side of the bridge for Ryan to come to him. Though perhaps it was as well he hadn't, as otherwise he might have been treated to the sight of Ryan fucking Sam Chancellor up against the nearest wall.

His tone wasn't lost on Cleaver, who drew himself up until pomposity was practically rolling off him. "I wondered if you'd had a chance to think over what we spoke about last night," he said, and tried very hard to make it sound conciliatory. That was belied by the look in his eyes, the one that said he hated having to play nice with Ryan.

"I can't do what you're asking," Ryan said shortly. Even if he could bring himself to ask and if for some reason his father agreed to hear him out, there was no guarantee his father would help. He was a businessman and he'd want an accounting of just how Cleaver had burned through the sizeable donation to Bessie's upkeep he'd made only three months ago. Ryan wouldn't mind knowing that too. It certainly hadn't gone on his wages.

Cleaver stiffened. Despite Ryan's refusal yesterday, he didn't seem to have expected this answer. Like Ryan's father, he wasn't used to being told no. "I'd advise you to think very carefully about that," he said. "I know keeping the train running is a labour of love to so many, but there are still very considerable expenses we have to meet. If we don't get some sort of injection of cash in the next week, I'm going to have to start making changes."

"That'd be a shame," Ryan said, because it was that or punch the guy. He didn't do well with being threatened. He sure as hell didn't do well with being threatened by a man who reminded him of his father, only without the intelligence and the sharp words that knew just how to slide their way between his ribs and lodge in his heart. "If there's nothing else, Mr Cleaver."

With a huff of annoyance, Cleaver turned his back and started to make his laborious way back up the footbridge. Ryan watched him go, and maybe it was as well the man was concentrating too hard on clutching the rail to get up those stairs to turn around, because he knew the hatred and impotent anger he felt were written all over his face.

He came back to himself when he heard a throat being cleared cautiously from a few yards away. Looking up, he found Sam standing there, looking apprehensive as he hunched slightly, like he was trying to hide.

"Is everything okay?" Sam's voice was uncertain.

The bark of laughter that escaped Ryan pretty much answered that—jeering and harsh. But then he looked at that dick Cleaver wheezing his way across the bridge, and came to a decision. He was out of a job anyway. He might as well have some fun before he went.

"You want to come and see Bessie?" he asked.

Sam's mouth dropped open, his cheeks grew pink and his eyes—God, he was like a golden retriever puppy who had been given his very own ball to play with.

"Really?" he breathed.

Ryan couldn't help it. Despite everything, he grinned at the pure shock and delight in Sam's face. "Really," he said. "Come on."

"But what about health and safety?" Sam asked, lengthening his stride to catch up with Ryan who was already moving towards the engine shed. "I thought only employees were allowed into the shed."

Well, yeah. But name one employee who loved that engine the way this kid did. If Ryan was on his way out anyway, he might as well give Cleaver a reason to get rid of him.

"Just don't tell anyone," he said, because he didn't give a shit about Cleaver, but if he ever wanted to work as an engine driver again, this couldn't get spread around among the trainspotting geeks. He glanced sideways at the excitement on Sam's face. Okay, so maybe he wasn't so much a geek as a cute, excited guy.

He went to the side door of the shed and got out his keys. Ritchie and Amit were long gone, having secured the carriages in the siding. It was just them. And Bessie.

When he opened the door and they stepped through, her presence struck him the way it did every single day. He remembered the first time he'd seen her. She'd been like a queen, mistress of all she surveyed, massive and powerful, sleek and beautiful. She was the embodiment of the sort of guy he wanted to fuck, but he tried not to think of her like that because that could lead to all sorts of embarrassing moments when driving her. The last thing he wanted was to develop some kind of fetish about trains.

Sam probably already had that fetish in spades. With a quick glance at Ryan to make sure he really was allowed, he crossed over to her and reached up to press a hand against her gleaming metal side.

"Hi, Bess," he said. His voice was supposed to be too low for Ryan to hear him, but it was filled with such love and warmth that he was glad he could hear it. Just yesterday Ryan would have laughed himself sick at the idea of a trainspotter wanting to *talk* to a train, but now he saw what it meant to Sam, he no longer felt the urge to laugh. Especially not when he remembered the way he always slapped her in greeting and farewell and most days said something to her as he did so.

He gave them a moment together, then climbed up onto the footplate. "You want to come up?" he asked.

It was the stupidest question ever asked, he realised, as Sam scrambled up after him, his face alight and eager. Gazing at the array of controls in front of him, Sam grinned until Ryan's face ached in sympathy. He couldn't seem to stop touching Bessie, his long, sensitive fingers caressing every part of her.

Somewhere in the back of his mind when he'd invited Sam to see Bessie, Ryan had thought about pushing him up against her and fucking him, because he was pretty sure Sam would be halfway to coming just from being so close to Bessie. But once he saw the delight in Sam's face as he looked around, those thoughts faded from his mind, especially when Sam wanted to know how she was to drive. Not just the nuts and bolts of it, but how it *felt*. How did he know deep inside that she was ready to start moving? Yes, there were all the gauges, but was there something more?

As Sam hung on his every word, warmth stirred inside Ryan at being the recipient of such open, genuine admiration. He couldn't remember ever being admired for anything except having a rich father or a good body, and the respect with which Sam seemed to regard him felt like spring sunshine after a long, hard winter.

He told Sam how she was a bit crabby first thing in the mornings, how sometimes her gauges said she was ready to go, but she still juddered as the wheels bit and held. And he told him something he'd never mentioned to another soul—the way she downright sulked when the carriages were first coupled to her, despite having more than enough power to pull them. It meant he had to nurse her those first few hundred yards until she got over it and seemed content to puff away happily.

Finally, they left the cab and after one final, slow, walk around her, Sam turned to Ryan. "Thank you," he said, and the depth of feeling in his voice was like nothing Ryan had ever heard before.

He shrugged. "No problem," he said as he locked the shed behind them. He didn't know what else to say. He wasn't going to confess that he'd actually enjoyed himself, because he couldn't remember the last time that had happened with another guy without it involving a lot of lube, sweat, and spunk.

While he hadn't forgotten how good Sam looked, forgetting to hunch his broad shoulders as he pored over every last inch of Bessie's innards, it somehow didn't feel right to proposition him here and now.

He was chewing at his lip as they walked back along the deserted platform, their shadows long and almost touching in the sinking sun. He wondered what the hell was wrong with him that, for the first time in his life, he couldn't find the words to ask if another guy wanted to fuck.

Chapter Four

SAM

"So, um, what you said yesterday?" Sam was flying high from being so close to Bess, from touching her and drinking in how it felt to stand on her footplate. He was determined to ride every bit of this feeling, which was giving him courage he'd never known before.

Ryan frowned, as if he was unsure what Sam meant. Sam didn't let that stop him, not today, not when he'd already had so much more than he thought he would. He was going for broke. The worst that could happen was Ryan would say no. The best that might happen was beyond his wildest dreams.

"About 'blowing off steam'," he said, his tone making it clear the phrase was in quotation marks because he still thought it was the corniest line he'd ever heard. And he watched a *lot* of porn so he heard a *lot* of corny lines.

Ryan's stride hitched, and then he halted completely, forcing Sam to stop and turn to face him. The look on Ryan's face wasn't the incredulity he'd half-feared but genuine amusement.

"You know, you were right," he said. "That's a bloody awful line."

The words were scarcely out of his mouth before he was moving forward. Having all of that predatory grace turned on him made Sam's mouth dry even as he swallowed reflexively. Because Ryan's eyes were intent on Sam's mouth, and he was swaying in closer and it was going to happen... Oh *God*, Ryan Saunders' lips were on his, soft and warm and utterly amazing.

Frozen for an instant, Sam didn't know what to do with his hands or his body or anything, but instinct—or Ryan—had his lips parting slightly. That was all that was needed for Ryan's tongue to slide inside. Sam's stomach twisted sharply at the slick warmth of Ryan's tongue against his, and he forgot everything except the desperate need for more.

He fisted his hands blindly in Ryan's overalls and pulled him close, opening his mouth further. He was making little sounds that were probably embarrassing, but Ryan Saunders was *kissing* him, and oh, *God*, his hands were on Sam's hips, tugging him in closer, and then on his arse, and Sam was so hard it hurt where Ryan's thigh was pressing between his legs.

"Fuck," Ryan said at last, pulling back, and his lips were wet and slightly parted and Sam couldn't stop staring at them. And then Ryan was rooting in the pocket of his overalls for the key to the staffroom. Sam, still speechless but harder than he'd ever been, was so close behind him as they piled through the door that he trod on the heel of Ryan's boot.

"Sorry," he started, but was cut off as Ryan pivoted and pushed him up against the wall, his muscular, perfect body pressing against him and his mouth back on his, his tongue pushing inside with renewed urgency and need. This time, Sam tried to kiss him back, and Ryan seemed to approve of this, tilting his head so he could slant his mouth more openly over Sam's, giving him better access.

He was so intent on Ryan's tongue in his mouth and how amazing it felt that Ryan's hand on his cock through his jeans caught him completely by surprise. He gasped and pushed against his hand, needing that touch so badly, and needing *more* as Ryan expertly worked his cock through the denim. It was only when Ryan gave a little laugh and stepped back slightly that Sam realised he'd been tearing at the zip on Ryan's overalls and pushing them down off his shoulders, desperate to get through the layers to *touch* Ryan.

"It's like that, is it?" Ryan said, taking a small step backwards and pushing the overalls down his legs before stepping out of them. But though he was teasing, there was no gainsaying the intensity in his eyes as he looked at Sam, or how hard his cock was where it pressed against the faded denim of his jeans.

Ryan stepped back in and there was more kissing, breathless and deep, slick and wet, and so damn good as Sam fumbled with Ryan's T-shirt, finally pulling it up until he could touch warm skin, which felt surprisingly soft under his touch. But however good that felt, it wasn't what he most wanted, and his hands were on the button to Ryan's jeans. He hesitated. He wanted to, but he wasn't sure if he should do this. If he was *allowed*.

"*Fuck*," Ryan said unevenly against his ear. "Do it."

Sam had always been good at doing as he was told. He eased the zip down over the bulge in those jeans, and as they opened he found Ryan was wearing black briefs that clung to the rigid line of his cock. His hand was unsteady as he reached out to stroke the hard length through the cotton. Ryan shivered, and that was all it took for Sam to work his hand into them and *finally* touch, feeling the length and the heat and the hardness.

He was shuddering, sure he was about come in his jeans. Ryan's hands were biting into his arms as Sam worked Ryan's jeans and briefs down around his thighs until all that was left was his dark, hard cock, jutting up proudly and making Sam ache with want. He thought if this were a porn flick, he would go to his knees now—and honestly, his mouth was watering at the thought of trying it, of having that gorgeous cock in his mouth, but he also knew he didn't have a clue what he was doing and he'd probably either choke himself to death or bite Ryan. Wrapping his hand around Ryan's cock was safer. It was like when he jerked himself off, only a million times better, feeling Ryan's thick erection.

Sam wanted it to go on forever, loving the warm weight in his hand, the way Ryan was breathing heavily at Sam's touch, but finally, with a muttered curse, Ryan froze, and wetness pulsed over Sam's hand.

"God," he muttered against Sam's neck.

It felt amazing to know that he'd brought Ryan Saunders off, but Sam didn't know what he should do next. He let go of Ryan's dick because if he was anything like Sam, he'd be sensitive as hell right now.

Thank God Ryan took over. His fingers curved around Sam's hand, calluses on his fingertips making Sam shiver openly as he realised they were from driving Bess, and raised it to his mouth. His eyes were steady on Sam's as he sucked one of Sam's fingers between his lips. Sam's knees nearly gave way at the feel of his hot, wet mouth sucking him, his tongue twisting so cleverly around his finger, and then he did the same with one finger after another until Sam's hand was cleaned of Ryan's spunk and he was about to explode inside his jeans with how hard he was.

Ryan moved back in against him, his breath hot, damp spurts against his neck as he drew Sam's zip down, the rasp of it almost as loud as Sam's rough breathing. And when Ryan's hand worked inside and *touched* him, the noise that wrenched out of Sam sounded like Bess when she was getting going in the mornings, a breathless, deep grunt.

He'd never known someone touching him would feel like this. It was nothing like when he touched himself. It was the difference between a toy train and Bess, with Ryan's calluses giving the most exquisite friction as his hand closed around Sam and started to pump him. And when Ryan's mouth closed over his, his tongue pushing inside as urgently as he was jerking him off, Sam was gone. Gasping and mindless, sounds breaking out of him as he lost it, clutching at Ryan desperately.

They stood there, heads bowed slightly, breathing fast and broken, and it was both the best moment of Sam's life and the most embarrassing, because his spunk was on Ryan's hand and on the floor, and he knew from how fast he'd come that Ryan must know the truth—that he was the first person ever to touch Sam like this.

Ryan picked his overalls up from the floor, wiping his hand on them before he scrubbed them briefly over the wetness on the lino.

"They need washing anyway," he said.

And then he rearranged himself and Sam followed suit until they were both decent again. Once they were done Sam leaned shakily back against the wall, not sure if his legs would carry him out of here. That was fine with him. He was quite happy to stay where he was for the rest of his life, reliving every moment of what he and Ryan had just done.

RYAN

Ryan might need to rethink his whole theory about Sam Chancellor being a virgin. Yes, he was inexperienced, but he was also eager as hell. If he was that abandoned when pushed up against a wall for a quick handjob, he'd be amazing in bed, laid out with space and time for Ryan to explore him properly, making those same little gasps he'd made as he'd shot everywhere. And then looked *mortified,* for God's sake, like this place hadn't seen all kinds of stuff over the years.

Not that Ryan had actually used it for this before—he hadn't thought there were any candidates here for a quick screw till he'd seen what lay beneath Sam's hoodie—but it was human nature. The combination of time to waste between trains and a large, squashy sofa that he avoided sitting on for that very reason meant the sign on the door might as well say "knocking shop" as "staffroom".

"You want to get that pint now?" he asked. Although he wanted more, even Ryan wasn't able to get it up again already, no matter what his press might say. And he didn't want to do it here. No, he wanted a big bed and privacy to lay Sam out and see just how eager he'd be with Ryan's cock deep inside him.

Sam was nodding, his eyes shining. There was no doubt that Sam wanted a second, proper round just as much as he did.

"You could—I mean, I've got beer at home. Only if you want," Sam said, blushing as if he was being too forward.

"You've just had your hand on my dick," Ryan pointed out. "It's not like inviting me back to your place is going to give me ideas. Unless you *do* mean just for a beer." In which case he might cry.

Sam's smile flashed out, the one that put dimples in his cheeks. "I hope not."

"Glad we've got that clear. So where do you live? Oh God, tell me you don't live with your parents or something." The whole nerd stereotype screamed that he probably did.

The smile dimmed slightly. "I live on my own," Sam said.

Thank fuck for that. Ryan's flat had the thinnest walls known to man, and the last thing he wanted was that snooty cow from next door banging on the wall just as things were getting good.

"So what are we waiting for?" he prompted, wanting to get them out of here and to a bed. It really had been too long since he'd had a good fuck. And no matter what Sam said about that line of his, he was like Bessie—if she didn't let off steam regularly, she'd blow. That was exactly how Ryan was with sex. It was a release when he could forget everything else in that frantic chase to the end, to that magic moment when pleasure ripped through him and everything stopped.

"Follow me," Sam said, a new confidence in his voice as he opened the door.

Ryan did, silently bemoaning the bagginess of Sam's jeans all the way.

SAM

Sam cudgelled his brains for something to say as they walked together past the closed ticket office—Val was long gone, thank God, because if she saw them together, she'd be bound to make some comment—and then turned up the street. They'd just done *that* together, so surely they could find something to talk about. He could ask about Bess until the end of time, but somehow he wanted to know about Ryan Saunders more than he did about Bess at the moment.

"How did you become an engine driver?" he asked at last, when the silence had started to get uncomfortable.

He got a sideways glance and a slight smirk. "Doesn't every kid want to be one when they grow up?" Ryan asked. "It was either that or an astronaut, but when I realised the astronaut would probably be a one-gig deal, I went with engine driver."

Sam smiled reflexively, but there was something in Ryan's voice under the answer, which had come out sounding so pat that he must say it frequently, that made him think he'd blundered onto a difficult subject.

"Are you new to Cardale?" he asked. "I mean, did you move here for the job or are you from around here?" That had to be a safe subject, surely.

Ryan glanced again at him, this time a hint of surprise in his face that Sam couldn't understand. He wasn't very used to this whole making-conversation thing, at least not with anyone under the age of seventy, and with Uncle Ken's friends the problem wasn't getting them talking but getting them to stop. Even so, he thought most people found something to talk about when they were getting to know one another.

"I came for the job," Ryan said. "It's too damn quiet here, but the views when Bessie gets out into the countryside make it worth it." His brow furrowed. "Have you ever actually ridden Bessie?"

"A couple of times," Sam said. "Once on my sixth birthday, and then when I first came to live here."

"You haven't always lived here?"

Sam shook his head as they turned into the long, straight street lined with terrace houses. "I came to live with my uncle—well, my great-uncle, really—when I was eleven," he said. "I lost my parents in a car crash."

It had become easier to say over the years, but he didn't think anything would ever take away the sorrow.

"Shit," Ryan said. "I'm sorry."

Sam shrugged. What else could he do?

"So where do you come from?" he asked, because if he didn't get the conversation back on track, it would falter into an awkward silence the way it always did after he told anyone about his parents. He snorted slightly as he realised what he'd asked. "Sorry, that makes it sound like you're from Mars or somewhere. I just meant, where did you live before here?"

"I've moved around a bit," Ryan said. "But I was in London right before coming here." He glanced around. "Cardale's a bit different," he said. "There's actually space to park outside people's houses."

Thankfully, before the conversation got any more laboured, they reached Sam's house. He led the way through the front door, which opened easily after a couple of days of dry, warm weather, and into the two-up, two-down house that had been built in Victorian times. Heading straight for the kitchen, he hoped to God that Ryan came up with a topic of conversation before things could get even more awkward.

He came out with a couple of cans of beer in his hand to find Ryan had shrugged off his jacket and put it over the back of the armchair. Sam glanced around, trying to see the room through a stranger's eyes, but it was simply *home*. Just as Uncle Ken had left it, only a little messier and perhaps in need of hoovering.

"So that's your pin-up," Ryan said, taking the beer from Sam.

Sam followed his gaze to the oil painting of the *Mallard* over the fireplace. "She's incredible, isn't she?" Sam asked as he stared reverently at her. "Uncle Ken once saw her and the *Flying Scotsman* on the same day at King's Cross, would you believe?"

"She's okay, I guess," Ryan said, and as Sam turned to look at him in indignation, Ryan put his beer down on the bookcase next to him. "But she's not exactly what I'm thinking about right now."

He moved towards Sam, who instinctively stepped back before realizing the predatory look in Ryan's eyes wasn't about violence. His stomach fluttered, his hand tightening on his beer as he looked around helplessly for something to do with the can.

Ryan solved that, plucking it from his hand and putting it on the bookcase beside his. "Where's the bedroom?" The promise in his low, sultry voice had Sam swallowing slightly.

"I—upstairs," he said, and hoped Ryan hadn't noticed the squeak in his voice.

"Lead on, Macduff."

For the second time that evening, Sam broke with the habit of a lifetime and led the way rather than shuffling along in someone else's shadow. His heart was thumping fit to burst as he climbed the stairs, aware of Ryan just behind him. Ryan wasn't touching him, not yet, but Sam was as sure as he could be that his eyes were firmly on Sam's arse.

The pounding in his chest meant he could hardly breathe by the time he pushed open his bedroom door, because this was really going to happen. He was really going to have sex. With Ryan freaking Saunders. Ryan Saunders, whose warm, muscular body was plastered against his back, while his crotch was pressed against his arse and making it very clear that Sam wasn't the only one who was excited at the prospect of what was going to happen.

Ryan's hands were under Sam's T-shirt, his roughened fingertips moved over his skin. When Ryan's fingertip skimmed over his right nipple, Sam shuddered all over, arousal twisting sharply deep in his stomach. Ryan's mouth was hot and wet on Sam's neck, but he suddenly stopped, leaving Sam dazed and wondering what he'd done wrong.

"Not that I'm fussy or anything," Ryan said, "but is there actually a bed somewhere under there?"

Sam finally saw what Ryan was staring at. Oh. After laying out practically every piece of clothing he owned this morning in his attempt to decide what to wear, he'd left them there in his rush to see Ryan again. His cheeks heated in embarrassment, but as Ryan's fingers traced a line on Sam's skin just above the waistband of his jeans, all embarrassment disappeared in the arousal that kicked through him.

He was a task-focused person. That was what Uncle Ken used to say. So he used that focus to suppress the shivers that Ryan's touch caused and instead yank the quilt, with all the clothes on it, onto the floor. That left the sheet-covered mattress ready and waiting for them. He turned back to face Ryan again, his stomach clenching tight at the look in his eyes.

RYAN

Whatever had sent Sam fleeing yesterday from the very suggestion of this had vanished and it seemed like he couldn't get enough of touching Ryan. Of kissing him, and it was weird because kissing didn't usually do much for Ryan, but something about the slick warmth of Sam's willing mouth, opening so easily for him, eager yet not greedy, was addictive.

He should be undressing Sam, except he'd got himself distracted by just how good Sam tasted and those wonderful little turned-on noises he was making as he squirmed against Ryan. His hands, which had finally found their way under Ryan's T-shirt, were a little uncertain and clumsy, but somehow they were more of a turn-on than the practised guys in the clubs because he *wanted* to touch Ryan, not just to hurry them along to the point where they could both get to it and come. Like half the pleasure was in the journey, not the destination.

He must have lost himself in tracing the muscles of Sam's back, feeling the way he shuddered at his touch as they kissed, because somehow Sam's hands were shy but firm on the button of his jeans. He was evidently unsure, waiting for permission rather than delving greedily inside, but nonetheless certain this was what he wanted.

Much as he wanted Sam's hand on his cock again—and he really did—Sam's enthusiasm had kind of taken over the situation. There wasn't the rush or urgency there'd been at the station, when they'd basically humped one another like teenagers. Now, with the edge taken off, Ryan could take longer to appreciate exactly what lay beneath Sam's T-shirt. He pulled it up by the hem and had to tug hard to get it over Sam's head.

When Sam finally emerged, his hair was even messier than usual and his cheeks were slightly pink. "It's a bit tight," he said.

"No shit," Ryan said, but then his voice dried because Sam…

Fuck, before he left here he was going to find every last shapeless hoodie in this guy's wardrobe and burn them, because his body was amazing. Ryan stared appreciatively. Sam's colour deepened as he did so, and Ryan realised it wasn't arousal—it was self-consciousness.

He leaned closer to take Sam's mouth in yet another kiss, and this time, when Sam opened eagerly beneath his lips and kissed him back, he swept his hands across the planes of Sam's back, feeling the smooth skin over his shoulder blades, the soft hollow of his back, and then his hands seemed to take on a mind of their own, curving down until they were on Sam's arse, tugging him tight against him. And yes, that arse was everything Ryan had remembered, firm and round and just *made* for Ryan's hands.

Thankfully Sam's jeans came off more easily than his T-shirt had, and it was the work of seconds to encourage him back onto the bed behind him. Sam went down so easily, so trustingly. Ryan knelt between his open legs—and God, the way he'd parted them so quickly and easily meant he was going to be heaven to fuck, so responsive and eager—and drank in the body in front of him.

Those legs were ridiculously long, but his pecs were delightfully firm with muscle, his abs were nice without looking like he lived in a gym, and thank fuck for that, because those kinds of guys were always more interested in themselves than anyone else. But along with the hoodies, Ryan was going to have to make a raid on Sam's underwear drawer because the faded, loose boxers he was wearing were hideous. The cock currently straining against them, its head dark and pushing up between the elastic and Sam's flat stomach, seemed to agree it wanted to be rid of them as soon as possible.

Ryan leaned down and mouthed at a sharp hipbone, Sam writhing and making a shocked sound as he did so, and carefully peeled off the bloody awful boxers and tossed them away somewhere, hopefully never to be found again. That left Sam's deliciously hard cock right in front of his face, and Ryan had never been one to miss an opportunity.

He leaned forward and, aware of Sam's responsiveness so far, thought to put his hands on Sam's hips before he ran his tongue slowly up the hot length of his cock. Thank fuck he did, because the way Sam jolted could have caused a nasty injury. He wouldn't want to have to explain that one at A&E—knocked out by a cock.

He looked up the bed to see Sam's head raised, his eyes very large and very dark, watching Ryan's every move as if he couldn't believe what he was seeing.

Suppressing a smile—because he might be a smug bastard, but it was probably better if he didn't actually *look* like one—Ryan slowly ran his tongue over the head of Sam's cock, licking at the wetness that was beginning to gather there. Then, holding Sam's disbelieving gaze, he slowly pushed his mouth down on Sam's hard cock.

Thank God Ryan was still holding his hips down, otherwise he'd have been choked to death. Sam was bucking up under him, writhing, making little bitten-off noises that sounded helpless and pleading as his fists clenched in the sheet beneath him. Better that than Ryan's hair, at least.

"God, please," he said. "*Ryan.*"

The rough wildness in Sam's voice, the way his throat was working as his body continued writhing had Ryan so hard he was rubbing himself against the sheet through his damn jeans, because somehow in undressing Sam he'd forgotten about himself. But he wasn't going to stop, not even to get his hand on his own cock, not yet, not when Sam tasted so good, *felt* so good, hard and hot and *big* in his mouth. He was making little sounds himself now, deep in his throat, swallowing them down the way he was swallowing around Sam's thick cock.

"*Ryan.*"

It was sharp and urgent. Ryan lifted his head and looked up at Sam, his lips throbbing and feeling swollen from what he'd just been doing. Sam was looking down the bed at him, chest heaving as he brought his breathing back under control.

"I was going to—I didn't want to come in your mouth," he said, shamefaced.

Ryan had give the kid points for manners.

He levered himself up to his knees, ignoring the disappointment on Sam's face as well as the lure of his cock, glistening wet from Ryan's mouth and its heavy curve so damn tempting. But no, he had plans. Sometime soon, he wanted Sam to come in his mouth, but right now, his own cock was demanding something more. Something like finding out just how tight that gorgeous arse was going to feel around him.

SAM

Being with Ryan this way felt like he'd been run over by the London express. From the instant he'd touched Sam, all Sam had been able to think was God, yes, please and *more*.

As for Ryan's mouth...he'd thought about it so often, but nothing he'd imagined had been as good as having a warm, slick mouth moving on him. And the fact it belonged to Ryan Saunders, his full lips stretched around Sam's cock, and the look of concentration on his face as his cheeks had hollowed, had Sam about to blow his load already. Which was completely understandable, but also just a bit embarrassing when Ryan wasn't even naked yet.

Thankfully that fact was about to get remedied. Ryan was stripping off his T-shirt—and of *course* it didn't get stuck as he pulled it over his head because that sort of thing only happened to Sam—and all coherent thought fled at what was revealed. Because even Sam's fantasies, and okay, so there'd been a *lot* of those after he'd first seen Ryan walking along the platform with that lazy stride of his that somehow was graceful and also drew attention to his hips, and arse, and, well everything—what was he saying?

Yeah. *That.* Lightly tanned smooth skin over wonderful muscle that Sam couldn't wait to touch. He sat up again, Ryan straddling his thighs, and all shyness fled with the *want* that filled him. He curved his hand around the back of Ryan's neck, feeling the short, fine hairs at the nape, and drew his mouth down to his. God, he could probably do this for the rest of his life, because kissing Ryan Saunders felt like nothing else on earth. *Touching* Ryan Saunders also felt like nothing else on earth, as Sam discovered when his fingers moved over the expanse of bare skin that had been revealed.

He explored it with a sense of wonder that he was allowed this, that Ryan was letting him. And then Ryan was pulling back slightly, his hazel eyes steady on Sam's as he undid his jeans, and Sam knew his tongue flicked out to moisten his lips as Ryan pushed them down his thighs. His hand stretched out to feel that rigid length through the black cotton, and Ryan made an approving little sound and pushed into his hand.

And suddenly, wonderful as this was, it wasn't enough. He wanted to wrap his hand around the silky warmth of his cock again. He eased the underwear down, and for a terrible instant thought he'd done something wrong because Ryan was moving off him. But he was only shifting to kick off his boots, followed by jeans and underwear, and then he was back on the bed, knees planted firmly either side of Sam's thighs as he pushed Sam down. The sense of predator was well and truly back. And Sam had never wanted to be prey as much as he did right now.

Ryan leaned forward, supporting himself on his hands, braced either side of Sam's biceps, and with the wickedest of smiles, lowered his hips until his cock was pressed against Sam's.

"Oh God!" It burst from Sam in a way that should have embarrassed him, but the feeling of Ryan's cock pressing against his, dragging and pushing and rubbing as Ryan slowly rolled his hips, was too much.

Maybe Ryan saw how close he was, because he paused in his movements. "Lube?"

"Bedside table," Sam said, and Ryan rolled off Sam long enough to reach out and open the drawer to snag the bottle. The rather empty bottle, Sam noticed with alarm. He'd been going through the stuff quicker than usual after Ryan had come to work at the station. But there was enough, surely, for now. There had to be, otherwise he'd die of disappointment.

"Condoms?" Ryan was still rooting around in the drawer.

Sam's face flamed. God. He hadn't even *thought*. He'd never bought any. He'd never had reason to. "I haven't got any," he said in a croak.

Ryan stopped molesting the drawer at that point to look at him. "I have," he said, and Sam could breathe once more.

But that didn't last long, because Ryan was leaning down off the bed, reaching for his jeans, which showed off his arse in the most enticing way. The muscles in his back were flexing as he reached out to snag the jeans, and Sam's hands seemed to have a mind of their own—they were following the movements of the muscles, and then it seemed purely natural to continue his explorations, until his hand was on Ryan's arse.

Sam's touch seemed to snatch the last of his self-control from Ryan because with a breathless curse he scrambled back onto the bed, putting a foil package down next to Sam's arm and picking up the lube once more. Sam wasn't sure what to do. This was so different from watching two actors going at it. It turned out he didn't have to lie there for long, agonised and wondering if he should be touching Ryan again or pulling him close or what, because Ryan had capped the bottle and was leaning forward, his lips meeting Sam's.

And it was so good, the slick tongue pushing between his lips, that it took him an instant to realise that Ryan's fingers were circling, and then one was—oh *God*, one of Ryan's strong, square fingers that had moved over Bess's controls with such assurance earlier was pressing inside Sam. He arched up, grunting slightly as his movement took Ryan's finger deeper.

He ripped his mouth away from Ryan's. "More," he demanded, and before he knew it he was filled, Ryan's fingers working in and out of him, and it was better than *anything*. All too swiftly, Ryan stopped what he was doing. Sam's protest was lost in his mouth as he leaned forward and stopped his disappointed complaint with a kiss that contained a hint of laughter.

"God, you're impatient," Ryan said as he pulled back and reached for the foil square on the bed.

Sam watched wide-eyed as he rolled the condom onto his hard cock with an ease that gave away just how often he did this, and Sam felt inadequate all over again because he didn't know what he should do. But when Ryan got his hands beneath his arse to lift him and started to press inside, he found his legs wrapping around Ryan's waist unbidden, as if his body knew exactly how to do this.

However good Ryan's fingers had felt, this was different. Big, and blunt and unforgiving and Sam gasped, because it hurt. It was too much. He couldn't do it. His hands were clenched tightly on Ryan's arms as Ryan paused, leaning over him, breathing hard as he looked down at Sam.

"Tell me when," he said.

Which would be *never*, except even though it hurt, Sam didn't want to lose this closeness with Ryan, so he just gripped tighter and concentrated on breathing.

And then Ryan leaned down and licked at his nipple, a hot swipe of his tongue that had Sam shivering. Either his movement or Ryan's changed something so that Ryan was sliding all the way in, big and hard, but it felt different now. Soft lips closed around his nipple before Ryan's teeth bit down and Sam bucked upwards, crying out with how it felt. Suddenly this wasn't only different, but *good*.

"God," he said, and he was grasping at Ryan, his hands scrabbling to find purchase on sweat-damp skin as Ryan held himself still, waiting, strain in his face betraying that he was having to force himself to wait.

"Fuck me." It came out low and filthy and as unlike Sam as it could possibly be, but he couldn't take it back. *Wouldn't* take it back, not when it felt so good as Ryan started to move inside him, big hard cock filling him, pushing inside him again and again until he was reaching with his hands and his body, close but not enough. His hand was on his cock and he was working himself, desperate, needing. Ryan shifted again, and Sam's legs were over Ryan's shoulders and Ryan was fucking into him so deep it hit him without warning, washing through him until he was coming so hard he thought he'd never stop.

He was still trembling from it when Ryan stiffened over him, a short, sharp whine forced between his teeth. And then he slumped down on top of Sam, breathing fast and rough against his neck.

"Fuck," he said as Sam clutched him, feeling the thundering of their hearts seeming to match one another, damp bodies against each other that should feel disgusting, especially as Sam was wet with more than just sweat, but right now it felt so good to have Ryan's body against his that he didn't care about anything else.

Long before he was ready to let go, Ryan was moving, pulling out of Sam. It took him a moment to realise Ryan was removing the condom from his dick. He flopped back on the bed as Ryan prowled across the room, the tied-off condom in his hand. Sam was grinning from ear to ear as he watched the perfection that was Ryan Saunders's naked arse leaving the room. He'd always known sex would be good, but he'd never expected it to be quite like *that*—kind of undignified and awkward at points, and really bloody *amazing*.

Sam was still grinning when Ryan came back. He stood in the doorway, looking confused. "Where the hell's your bathroom?"

"Downstairs," Sam said. As Ryan frowned in incomprehension, he thought he'd better explain. "When the house was built, there was just an outside privy. Uncle Ken had to put an extension on for the bathroom."

"There's no bloody way I'm walking half a mile clutching a used condom looking for your bathroom," Ryan said, but somehow the outrage in his voice didn't sound too serious. "Where's your damn bin?"

As he asked, he spotted it in the corner of the room and dropped the offending condom in. Sam thought he should think that was kind of gross, but he was too happy right now to worry about stuff like that. He was still grinning inanely when Ryan turned round to face him.

RYAN

Ryan hated condoms. Well, not really, except for when he did. Like just now, when he'd come so hard he'd wanted nothing more than to collapse on the bed next to Sam and drift in that peaceful feeling of satisfaction.

Coming was usually like scratching an itch or squeezing a spot—a moment of release and relief that was glorious but fleeting. Forgotten as soon as it was done. This had been good. Better than good. Sam had been a bit clumsy, long arms and legs that he didn't seem to know quite what to do with, but willing and welcoming. Having to get up and deal with the condom was a bit of a mood-killer.

When he turned back and saw Sam leaning to scrabble at the duvet, shaking it out to dislodge the piles of clothes before pulling it onto the bed, and he saw the dimples carved deep in his cheeks by his smile, and the happiness in his eyes, he wished even more he could have stayed collapsed next to Sam for just a few minutes. Instead, he'd have to pull his clothes on and get going, leaving Sam looking like some sort of happy, gigantic dormouse curled up under his duvet.

But then Sam was lifting up a corner of the covers in invitation, and there was nothing in his face that gave away he knew he was breaking the casual-fuck rule so thoroughly. But neither was there anything in his face that had Ryan wanting to run—the usual sort of calculation about how rich he was and how best to snag him.

In a moment of weakness, he slid under the duvet next to Sam. And instantly regretted it as their elbows and knees knocked together. It turned out Sam was a bed hog.

"Budge over," he demanded, elbowing Sam in the side.

Sam shifted enough to allow an extremely emaciated string bean room to lie down, at which point Ryan poked him in the ribs with a finger, to find Sam jack-knifed with a high-pitched giggle. Ryan, never one to miss an opportunity, decided to make a bid for more bed and started to tickle him in earnest. It ended up with Sam gasping under him, tears in his eyes and a look of helplessness on his face oddly similar to the way he'd looked as he'd come. His mouth was open as he gasped for breath in between pleading with Ryan to stop, and it seemed the most natural thing in the world for Ryan to lean down and kiss him again.

And just so long as Ryan kept his hands away from Sam's ribs, because nearly getting kneed in the balls taught him that lesson pretty quickly, it turned out Sam was very happy to be kissed. And then the bed was more than big enough for two while the room slowly grew dark around them.

Chapter Five

RYAN

Ryan woke with a start, heart thumping as deafening noise blasted in his right ear. Completely disoriented, it wasn't until the figure next to him stirred and batted a long arm in the direction of the beside table that he remembered where he was. And oh shit, that was daylight through the open curtains. He knew he hadn't slept well the night before, but this was ridiculous—he must have slept from nine through to...

"What's the time?" His voice was deep and hoarse.

Sam, who'd flopped back down on the pillow next to him, opened an eye. Yesterday's sweet-tempered look was nowhere to be seen. "Too early," he muttered, then sighed and obviously made a Herculean effort. "Six."

Just as well it was a Thursday, the day set aside for maintenance, or he'd be late. He threw the covers back, ready to get out of bed. Sam turned over next to him, grumpily thumping his pillow until he was lying with his back to Ryan, his spine a stiff, annoyed line.

"What time do you need to leave?" Ryan asked, wondering whether Sam should hit the shower first. If questioning him meant he had to push up close to Sam and run his hand lightly down the warm curve of his arm, while his cock nudged insistently at that firm, rounded arse, well, that wasn't his fault. And from the way Sam's body relaxed and he moved backward slightly, pressing against Ryan's morning wood, he was performing a public service, getting the kid to like mornings.

"Not yet," he murmured, and unless Ryan was mistaken, the thickness in his voice wasn't because he'd just woken up but because of the way Ryan's hand was mapping the lines of his chest, running over a nipple and making sure to catch it with the edge of his nails before exploring further south. Sam's belly quivered slightly at his touch, and then Ryan found the line of hair that led downwards, until he wrapped his hand around the heat of Sam's cock, already hard and ready.

He rolled his hips against Sam's arse, rubbing off against that smooth skin as he worked Sam in a way that had Sam flailing behind him to grasp Ryan's arse and pull him even closer. The strength in him was deliciously promising for the future, but for now there was just the press of flesh against flesh, harsh breathing and Sam gasping as he writhed, caught between Ryan's hand and his cock, pressing back and forward and losing it with a suddenness that took Ryan by surprise.

And then he turned around and touched Ryan's cock, a slight uncertainness apparent until Ryan wrapped his hand around Sam's and showed him just how he liked it. Sam was a bloody quick learner, because it wasn't long at all before Ryan was swearing and coming, his spunk spilling hot and wet between them.

Before he could flop back onto the pillow the way he wanted—the way he *needed* to—Sam's fucking alarm clock blasted again. At this rate Sam was going to kill Ryan from a heart attack, one way or the other.

SAM

Sam poured boiling water into his breakfast mug, hesitating for a moment over the second mug. He decided to wait till Ryan had finished his shower before making him some tea. Assuming he wanted it, of course.

He had no clue how these casual hookups worked, but if he'd thought about it, he would have expected Ryan to leave after they'd had sex last night, not stay the night. And it wasn't in a creepy way, like he was trying to move in or anything—he'd seen *that* porn flick too, and *Misery* had nothing on the things the stalker had got up to.

But no, it was just like they were friends—him and Ryan Saunders. He snorted at how ridiculous that sounded and prodded hopefully at the teabag with a teaspoon, willing it to be ready.

"Bloody *hell*!"

He jumped as Ryan rocketed out of the bathroom and stood in the kitchen doorway, looking distinctly wild-eyed.

"What?" he demanded, catching Ryan's panic.

"You've got fucking *Shelob* in your shower," Ryan said. He headed for the living room. "I'm getting my boots so I can stomp it."

"*No!* It's just Mabel," Sam protested, heading towards the bathroom as fast as he could go because the thought of Ryan squashing her was unbearable. "She's here most mornings," he explained, crouching down by the shower tray where, sure enough, Mabel the house spider had reclaimed her usual corner after Sam's swift shower. "I put her outside when I remember, but come the next day, she's always back again. I think she likes it here."

Scooping her up and holding her gently but firmly, because he'd discovered the hard way she'd escape if she possibly could, Sam returned to the kitchen and unlocked the back door. Ryan was there, but for every step Sam took, he retreated a pace, eyes fixed suspiciously on Sam's cupped hand.

"She wouldn't hurt anyone," Sam said before turning his attention to Mabel. "Would you, sweetheart?"

"Yeah, right. Have you seen the *size* of that thing?" Ryan said. "They bite, you know."

"So do you," Sam pointed out, because there was a red mark on his neck from Ryan's mouth. He stiffened as he realised he'd just been rude.

To his relief, Ryan snorted a laugh. "Just get rid of it."

Sam went out into the garden and set Mabel down amid the nasturtiums, like usual. She scuttled off, like usual. He wondered sometimes what she did during the day when he was at work. Probably plotted new ways back into the bathroom.

"You grow all this shit?"

He looked up to find Ryan standing in the doorway, surveying the small garden behind the house. The beans were beginning to climb the poles, and then there were the cabbages that he rarely ate because he didn't really like cabbage, but it felt right to have them there as Uncle Ken had always grown them in that patch.

He shrugged, a bit embarrassed at the surprise in Ryan's voice. "I guess," he said, because it wasn't like he could say Mabel did the gardening.

Ryan's eyebrows rose. "That's pretty cool."

Sharp rapping sounded on next-door's window, and Sam realised that Ryan was stark naked. "Oh my God," he said, and pushed Ryan back inside, closing the door firmly behind them. "I think you've just given Miss Harbottle a heart attack."

"Or the best day of her life," Ryan said with a smirk. The same smirk that he so often wore and which should make him seem insufferable but somehow didn't.

He retreated into the bathroom while Sam poured his cereal and had his tea. Ryan emerged, sadly fully dressed, when Sam was chasing the last bits of cereal round his bowl.

"Cup of tea?" Sam offered.

Ryan shook his head. "I need to get to work," he said, then paused and stared at the box of cereal on the counter. "Frosties?" he asked. "Seriously? I didn't know they still made them."

Sam stared at him in surprise because of *course* they still made them. Why wouldn't they? And he always had them. He had ever since his first morning here when Uncle Ken had gone out and bought the most sugary, child-friendly cereal he could find in his attempt to make a lost and devastated kid feel at home. Uncle Ken hadn't had children of his own and didn't spend a whole lot of time around them, but he'd turned his life upside down to give Sam a home.

"I like them," he said defiantly, and swallowed the last pieces on his spoon before putting it down with a clatter and staring at Ryan, his chin up.

"Hey, okay." Ryan backed off, hands up in surrender. "I was just surprised. I should get going anyway."

"Yeah, me too," Sam said, because if he didn't get moving, he was going to be late. He paused awkwardly. "I'd offer you a lift, but I usually catch the bus. Means I don't have to worry about parking."

"It's okay," Ryan said. He was putting his boots on, kneeling to lace them up, causing his jeans to pull across the muscles in his thighs. Thighs which Sam knew intimately now. He knew what they felt like under his hands and how it felt when those muscles worked as Ryan pushed into him.

He swallowed, his mouth dry, before remembering he had a job to get to. He tore his gaze away from Ryan and put his own shoes on.

When they left the house, he knew it wasn't his imagination that Miss Harbottle's net curtain twitched as they walked past her house. He couldn't blame her. This was the first visitor he'd had since Uncle Ken had passed who was younger than fifty. He was also the first who was good looking, who stayed the night and who showed up naked in his kitchen the next morning.

Sam was grinning as he walked next to Ryan in the spring sunshine. He still couldn't believe what had happened, but the proof was walking next to him. He'd had sex. With another person. And not just any other person, but the most sexy guy he'd ever seen. Who hadn't just been satisfied with a quick fuck, but had stuck around afterwards.

"Where do you work?" Ryan's voice brought Sam back from his daydream, and what was he *thinking*? He'd have all the time in the world to relive what had happened once Ryan had gone. He should be grabbing at every moment of this while he still could.

"Braddons," he said. "The big department store in the square."

Ryan's brow furrowed slightly, then cleared again as he evidently placed Braddons. "I'm surprised a place like that's still going with all the chain stores."

Sam nodded. Ryan wasn't the only one to think that way. "I guess a lot of the older people in town have always shopped there, so they still do."

But that wouldn't last forever, and maybe one day Braddons would be gone too. Almost everyone Sam knew in this town was over sixty, but that wasn't a fair representation of the town's population, so somewhere like Braddons couldn't keep going indefinitely.

It was just that Sam's friends were all Uncle Ken's friends. Sam hadn't made any friends at school because by the time he'd come to Cardale, everyone else had already established friendships. In any case, no one wanted to be seen with the awkward guy who all the bullies picked on. Now he didn't have a clue how to make any new friends. He'd told himself he was happy with his online friends because at least he could talk trains to them. But somehow having Ryan walking beside him and idly chatting felt even better than being on the forum did.

Except that as Ryan peeled off at the station with a nod to Sam and a casual, "See you", he thought he shouldn't get used to it. It had been blowing off steam, and nothing more than that.

He glanced at his watch and lengthened his stride. He would have all the time in the world later to go over everything they'd said and done together. For now, he had a bus to catch.

RYAN

Halfway through the afternoon, Ryan was ready to go home. He usually enjoyed Thursdays, even though a lot of it was messy, backbreaking work under the eagle eye of the qualified mechanic who made sure Bessie was never at anything less than her best. But today he'd had enough of oiling and greasing parts of her as Simon emptied the pit into which he cleared the ash pan every day.

Surely in this day and age at least some of this stuff could be done by machine. But no, Cleaver was too tight to shell out on anything just to make other people's lives easier. And the mechanic, Jim, who'd been here every Thursday since Ryan had started this job, was out sick today. His replacement, who'd introduced himself as Mr Perkins, evidently possessing no first name, was a royal pain in the arse. Ryan had no problem with things being done properly—he insisted on it when it came to Bessie—but Perkins seemed more intent on doing things the correct way than in understanding the reasoning behind them. Form over substance, Ryan's father would have said.

"What the blazes?"

Ryan looked up from where he was checking the side-rod oiling points and trying not to think about other places he'd rather be applying lubrication right now, all of which involved some vaguely formed idea about laying Sam Chancellor out on his bed once again and fucking him within an inch of his life. Perkins's hectoring voice had changed in pitch and he sounded truly shocked, not the counterfeit version he'd been trying on them all day when he found out their working practices. It was that attitude which had made Simon volunteer to dig out the ash pit, just to get away from him.

"What?" he asked. No matter how much of a dickhead this guy was, if it was about Bessie, he needed to know.

"Who's been doing your weekly checks?" Perkins asked, eyes concentrated on whatever it was that had got his attention.

"Jim," Ryan said.

"Well, that's *very* helpful," Perkins snapped.

"Well, I don't know his damn name. He's from your company. Why the hell don't *you* know?"

Perkins sniffed and turned his attention back to Bessie.

"What is it?" Ryan asked.

"The brake shoes are wearing the wheels down to scrappage level," he said.

"Shit." Ryan straightened up and strode over to where Perkins was examining one of the wheels. "How bad is it?"

"Bad. And they're flanging on the edge of the wheel."

"I know they're overhanging a bit, but they've got all the surface contact they need," Ryan pointed out, because the last thing he needed was for Bessie to be taken out of service for a not-yet-due major overhaul. It would take so long that he'd be out of a job even if Cleaver didn't follow through on his threat to sack him. A threat which he'd managed to forget about while screwing Sam Chancellor but which was now well and truly back on his mind.

"It's a case of regulations," Perkins said stiffly.

Ryan managed—*just*—not to give voice to what he thought of regulations and the blind adherence this guy insisted upon. He watched instead as Perkins measured very carefully.

"Well," Perkins said at last. "I suppose it's *just* within tolerance, but it's not optimal."

"So she can still run?"

"Yes, but I'll be making a note in my report," Perkins said. "Haven't you finished servicing the grease points yet?"

"Fuck you," Ryan muttered under his breath as he turned away. He didn't do well with authority. He certainly didn't do well with authority wielded by someone who was so self-important they practically disappeared up their own backside. And all because he had some fancy degree that Ryan didn't. The guy was probably a virgin and that was why he was so uptight.

As Ryan crouched back down by Bessie, he stilled. Because that was what he'd thought about Sam, but then they'd got so into it that he'd forgotten. Fuck. He dropped his head forward and stared blindly at his boots. Sam certainly hadn't been very experienced, but had Ryan really been his first? Because if so, he would have done things a bit differently. Not that it hadn't been good—it had been very, *very* good, showing just how long it had been since he'd last got laid—but he might have taken a bit more time instead of just going for it. Sam hadn't seemed to mind, though.

He grinned at the memory of Sam writhing under him, his long body moving restlessly as demands for more spilled from his mouth. If Sam *had* been a virgin, he hadn't been a shy, blushing one. Maybe he just hadn't had the opportunity rather than any other reason. And looking at the way he dressed and the way he moved, Ryan could see how he faded into invisibility.

"Saunders? How much longer are you going to be? I need to get on the road before the rush hour."

He bit back the response that rose to his lips and concentrated on Bessie again.

SAM

"They're medium flow pads, not panty liners," Melanie said, her usual calm manner shredded. "Honestly, Sam—what's with you today? You've had your head in the clouds ever since you got here. If Beaky sees you got the shampoo and conditioner mixed up, he'll have your guts for garters."

Sam actually *looked* at the stuff he'd brought down from the stock room. Melanie was right—at least half the things on the trolley weren't what he'd gone upstairs to get.

"Damn it," he said. "Sorry. I'll go back up."

"I'll do it myself," Melanie said. "Goodness only knows what you'll come back with this time." She tilted her head on one side. "Seriously, is everything okay?"

He nodded, though he suspected the heat in his cheeks meant he was blushing. Every time he moved, some part of his body seemed to remind him of what he'd done the previous night. It was hard to turn his mind to anything else when all he wanted to do was remember everything that had happened and how it had felt. He'd always known he'd like sex, but he'd never understood just how different the touch of someone else's hands on him would feel.

"Watch the till for me, there's a dear," Melanie said. "Beaky doesn't like it if I'm off the floor."

Beaky was Melanie's nickname for the pharmacist who ran this department with a rod of iron. Most of the time Sam didn't mind the man's attitude because he did his job quietly and well and so never got on his wrong side, but today his head was everywhere except where it needed to be.

Then again, it wasn't like he was an engine driver, not like Ryan, responsible for something as rare and precious as Bess. He didn't think the world would come to an end if he put the peppermint toothpaste out with the spearmint, no matter what Beaky might think.

When he got home at the end of the longest day he could remember, Sam didn't follow his usual habit of putting the kettle on for a cup of tea, but instead went up to his bedroom. He wanted some sort of proof that what he remembered had *really* happened. The messy piles of clothes still on the floor from where he'd shaken them off the quilt assured him that it hadn't all been some wonderful, vivid dream. He really had had sex. With Ryan Saunders.

He took off his tie and shirt in front of the full-length mirror and stared at himself. There were still marks on his neck from Ryan's mouth. He unzipped the smart slacks he wore for work, and when they fell down and pooled around his ankles, he could see bruising on his hipbones. The marks were light, but a shiver ran through him as his fingers lingered on his left hip. It was as if by touching the darkened skin, he could feel Ryan's hands on him again—so strong and sure, yet careful too. Sam had thought he'd known what to expect from sex after all the porn he'd watched, but he hadn't been prepared for how intimate it would feel to have someone do those things to him.

Goose bumps raised on his skin, and he shook his head slightly, bringing himself back to here and now. Stepping out of his slacks, he picked a pair of jeans off the floor and slid into them. Wonderful as it had been—and it *had* been, even more than his wildest dreams, having someone who didn't see Sam as the gay nerd who'd spent half his teenage years with his teeth in braces, just to seal his fate as least popular kid in the class—it wasn't going to happen again. Not with Ryan, anyway. If he wanted it to happen again with someone else, he'd have to change things. He'd have to make it happen.

But not yet. Right now, he was going to drift along in the afterglow of the best night of his life. And if wanting reminders of it meant not picking his clothes up or changing the sheets yet, he could live with that. That might be kind of disgusting of him, but it wasn't like anyone would ever know.

RYAN

Ryan had a hot shower when he got back to his flat. He stayed under the water long after the dirt had been washed away, hoping the tensions of the day would also disappear down the plughole.

The day had gone to hell quicker than he could imagine. Perkins wanted to see a whole load of changes by the end of next Thursday, otherwise he'd threatened he wouldn't sign off on Bessie being safe. And every single one of those changes would cost money, whether it was replacing parts or work that only Simon and Ryan could do, meaning there'd be an overtime bill for Cleaver to pay. And he wouldn't pay it, that was damn clear. He *couldn't* pay it, if he was to be believed. That couldn't be right, because Bessie cost a fortune to run, but the crowds she pulled in and the price they paid for tickets brought in a tidy sum, and Ryan had some idea of just how much his father had donated to her upkeep just a few months ago.

He'd do the work as a one-off for free if it meant keeping his job and keeping Bessie running, but he was pretty sure that setting a precedent like that meant Cleaver would refuse to pay them for any extra work in the future. And much as Ryan loved driving Bessie, he wasn't going to be a slave for anyone. He still had a life outside work.

Though, as he turned the shower off and caught himself swiftly glancing into the corners of the wetroom, checking for lurking gigantic spiders after this morning's episode, he realised he didn't. Not any more. He'd left his life behind in London, and all there was for him here was Bessie and a flat he probably shouldn't have bought because everyone else in the converted Georgian house was snooty as hell. They didn't like the fact his fingers sometimes left oil stains on the front door, let alone that "death machine" he rode, because "motorbikes lowered the tone" of the place, or so that snooty cow next door had been saying to an overdressed friend when he'd come down the stairs one morning and found them gossiping in the hallway.

He'd greeted them with a drawled, "Morning, ladies," and subjected them both to a good eye-fucking before sauntering out with a swing of his hips, leaving them speechless and gasping, though he still wasn't sure if it was outrage or because they were turned on. He guessed they weren't sure either.

Fuck them. Fuck Cleaver and fuck this town, because if he had to leave, if he lost this job, he didn't know what the hell he'd do. There was only one thing he was qualified for—the downside of having been expelled from every school he'd been in after the age of fourteen, until he'd hit sixteen and emptied his savings account to take himself off to Bali when his classmates were sitting their exams. He guessed he could sell the flat and go travelling again. It felt like running away, though, not embarking on an adventure, even though he didn't know what he was running away from.

Fuck it. He pulled on some ripped, faded jeans and an old band T-shirt and scrubbed his hair with a towel before using just enough product for it to look like its usual self rather than the rat's nest of Sam Chancellor's hair. His lips quirked at the thought of someone as hopelessly out of touch with clothes and hairstyles as Sam was being so hot under it all. Most guys with a body that good would be flaunting it.

He turned slightly so he could check out his arse in the mirror. He might be pushing thirty, but he'd still got it. He should go out and get laid again. That would take his mind off everything else. It had certainly worked last night—he'd lost himself in those long arms and legs wrapped tightly around him as Sam had writhed under him, desperate for his cock.

The problem with this bloody town was knowing where to go. He still hadn't discovered a gay pub, despite trying most of them during his first few weeks here. And he didn't want to go for a Grindr hookup because for that to work the other guy had to be at least attractive, and in a small town like this, he hadn't seen much worth checking out. Though if they were all as invisible as Sam Chancellor had been before Ryan had actually *looked* at him, maybe that was why.

He hesitated, bike keys in his hand. He was on his way *somewhere*, that was clear. He couldn't stay here all night because he knew the emptiness filling him wouldn't let him sleep. Last night he'd had a distraction and had slept the best he could remember in years. And that was despite sharing a bed, something he didn't usually like doing. He liked his space, his freedom, not the length of Sam Chancellor's warm body against his.

As he remembered how it had felt, he hesitated. He never did this. He wasn't that pathetic guy—he was the one they always chased. But this wasn't chasing. This was merely because there was no one else, and it wasn't like Sam was the sort who'd judge him for it. He'd been different from anyone else Ryan could remember—honest, and open, and underneath the shyness, stubborn as hell.

He remembered the way Sam's chin had come up at Ryan's slight against his breakfast cereal and snorted with sudden laughter. And then he remembered the same face, cheeks flushed, lips parted and dark eyes full of hunger and pleasure as Ryan had slid into him.

He was out of the door before he knew it. He could always claim he'd lost his phone and wanted to know if it was at Sam's. He was pretty sure Sam wasn't experienced enough to see through the lie.

The only problem was going to be remembering which in that long row of identical houses was Sam's. Ryan might have swallowed his pride enough to knock on his door, but he wasn't going to be pathetic enough to knock on more than one door, looking for the right house. If he didn't find it the first time, he was out of there.

Chapter Six

SAM

Sam stuffed the last piece of cheese on toast into his mouth and licked his fingers. He didn't want to get grease on the keyboard of his laptop, not now he was finally logged in to the forum and catching up on all he'd missed the previous night. To his surprise, it wasn't as much as he'd expected. Quickly skimming through the messages posted, he could see that the Hereford train was still the main topic of conversation, but other than that, nobody had much to say. Nobby was off on his holidays soon, touring Scotland's West Highland Line, and he was full of excitement about that, while two of the other forum regulars were sharing photos from the weekend trip they'd taken to Didcot Railway Centre.

In the past, Sam had read these sorts of posts with a wistfulness that bordered on envy. He enjoyed hearing about their adventures, but they reminded him of what he couldn't have. Tonight, the familiar feelings of longing sputtered out into nothingness as it dawned on him—he *could* do it. There wasn't a single thing stopping him taking himself off on holiday on his own. He could afford it. Uncle Ken had left him the house, mortgage-free, and it wasn't as if he spent his wages on anything. If he sat around here waiting for someone to turn up to go with him, he'd spend the rest of his life staring at his laptop. But he didn't want to go on holiday on his own.

Maybe he should sign up for a dating website. Except if he mentioned trains as an interest, let alone that they were his major hobby, everyone would run far and fast, and he wasn't going to hide something that was such an important part of his life. He sighed, raking a hand through his hair. Maybe it was for the best. Maybe now wasn't the right time to go looking anyway, because who on earth out there could live up to Ryan Saunders?

Sam knew he'd never catch the attention of anyone as sexy as Ryan or as kind as he'd turned out to be—he hadn't once laughed at Sam for not knowing what he was doing. He'd just seemed to roll with it, letting Sam know what he liked and what he wasn't so keen on by covering his hand where he'd had it curled around Ryan's cock and guiding him in the rhythm he'd wanted.

Just the memory of it, of the hard, silky heat in his hand, of the intensity in Ryan's eyes, of the way his full lips had parted as he'd breathed more heavily, had Sam half-hard. He opened another tab in his browser to go to his favourite porn site, but then hesitated. It would never be as good again, just watching, not now he knew how it felt. Maybe he should stop watching and start doing.

His cheeks were hot as he typed in his search term. When he followed a link, they stayed heated, but this time it wasn't at his ignorance. It was at the "instructional" video of how to give a blowjob, which was the hottest thing he'd ever seen now that he knew it actually felt.

He was making mental notes the whole time, and when the video finally finished, he clicked one which dealt with the whole spit or swallow dilemma and had to adjust himself in his jeans. He kept imagining what it would have been like if he'd had the courage to try this last night.

The sound of the doorbell had Sam jumping a mile, heart hammering in his chest, as he slammed down the laptop lid. He felt like a small child caught with his hand in the biscuit tin. And then he wondered who it could possibly be—none of Uncle Ken's friends ever called this late in the evening. It had to be Jehovah's Witnesses or someone wanting to sell him double-glazing.

With a last guilty glance at his laptop, sitting innocently on the couch, he adjusted himself again so his erection was less obvious and went to answer the door.

RYAN

Ryan had pulled into the side of the street at about the place where he thought Sam's house was. Having turned off his engine, he sat there for a moment, wondering whether he should just start the bike up again and go. Except all that would be waiting for him in his flat would be more thinking, and he couldn't crack open a bottle of something to take his mind off things because he knew damn well he'd drink more than he should and he wasn't going to risk driving Bessie tomorrow with a blood alcohol count. Given that his short-lived career was heading for the buffers just as fast as it could go courtesy of Cleaver, it wasn't the thought of getting sacked that stopped him. It was the thought of Bessie getting damaged on his watch if he made a mistake, not to mention he was responsible for the safety of all the families stuffed into her coaches.

He pulled his helmet off and swung off his bike. He'd give this one try. If he couldn't find Sam's house straightaway, he'd drive to the nearest city and go to a club. He wasn't exactly dressed for it, but old jeans and a T-shirt would have to do. And if he spent long enough screwing some twink's brains out, he wouldn't be tempted to drink or try anything harder that might be doing the rounds.

The houses were practically identical. They were Victorian terrace houses with bow windows, each front door painted in a dark colour with a small stained-glass window overhead. He hadn't a clue what colour Sam's front door had been last night. He'd been too busy looking at Sam's arse, so far as he could through those jeans.

But then he saw it—the stained-glass window in front of him showed a steam engine puffing across the top of the door. No doubt about it—this had to be Sam's house. Ryan was grinning as he rang the bell. Seriously, Sam had to be the geekiest trainspotter there ever was.

When Sam answered the door, any thoughts about geeky went straight out of Ryan's head. Okay, Sam's hair was still as much a mess as ever, but his lips opened in a little gasp of surprise as he saw Ryan and instantly put filthy thoughts into Ryan's head about how he'd look with his mouth stretched around Ryan's cock, just before Ryan pulled out at the last instant and came all over his face, stringing white spunk across his mouth and cheeks until he had to lick it off his lips. And then there was the bulge that even the tragedy of his jeans wasn't hiding completely. He remembered Sam's cock being a very nice size indeed, but it wasn't *that* big. Not unless he was hard.

"Am I interrupting?" he asked. He *knew* he was smirking, but this was priceless—had he just walked in on Sam Chancellor having a wank? And the kid had still been good-mannered enough to answer the bloody door. Was he for real?

"I—uh—do you want some cheese on toast?" Sam stammered, and then his cheeks flushed fire-engine red. If he hadn't looked so cute, Ryan would have laughed himself sick.

"Sounds good," he said, and when Sam moved back to let him in, he walked past Sam, closer than was strictly necessary. He heard Sam swallow. He should get a medal for *not* reaching out to cup the hardness at his crotch. Instead, he bent over and started undoing his boots. He'd always been taught to take his shoes off when going to someone else's house. It was nothing to do with wanting to tease them both by flaunting his arse at Sam.

"I'll—just—yes," Sam muttered, and fled in the direction of the kitchen.

Ryan grinned, heeled off his boots, shucked off his jacket and followed him.

SAM

Cheese on toast? Cheese on bloody toast? Who *did* that? Sam Chancellor, apparently. Who currently wanted to die. Because this was Ryan bloody Saunders, and all Sam could think was to offer him cheese on toast. He stood in the kitchen, staring at the loaf of bread on the breadboard and trying not to hyperventilate.

"So, cheese on toast?" Ryan said with a grin that was both mocking and not, which meant Sam had no option but to pick up the breadknife.

The slices he cut were more like doorsteps than slices, but with a hard-on the size of the Eiffel Tower in his jeans, he reckoned he was doing well to cut bread at all. Maybe the Eiffel Tower was a bit of an exaggeration, but it certainly felt huge enough to be all but doing the can-can in front of Ryan to ensure he'd noticed it. The way Ryan was leaning back against the sink, his arms crossed in a way that pulled his ancient-looking AC/DC T-shirt tight across his chest and put every muscle in his arms on display as he watched Sam, wasn't helping his problem to subside.

Sam stuck the bread under the grill, got the cheese out of the fridge and cut some slices. They were slightly thinner than the bread, but not by much. By the time the toast was ready to be turned over and have cheese put on it, he wanted to cry with how much he needed to touch himself, to *do* something about the hard-on straining in his underwear, but he couldn't do a thing under Ryan's watchful gaze.

"Do you want Marmite on it?" he asked instead. Anything to take his mind off how tempted he was to go into the bathroom, unzip himself and wrap his hand around his cock.

"Marmite? Are you insane?" The outrage in Ryan's voice jerked Sam away from thoughts of his dick. "That stuff tastes like the Devil crapped it out."

"That's disgusting," Sam said, his nose wrinkling at the image Ryan had conjured. He peered at the cheese, which was starting to melt nicely, and spread it around a bit with a knife. "Nearly done," he said, and was he *really* about to serve Ryan Saunders cheese on toast? What was Ryan doing here anyway? Sam wanted to think it was to see him, but they hadn't said anything about seeing one another again, and it wasn't exactly likely.

"I—er, not that it's not—I mean, it's nice to—but why—oh God." Sam was saved as the cheese on the piece closest to him started bubbling wildly, as if it was going to burn any second. He switched the grill off and put the slices on plates. "There you go," he said instead, and pinched himself *hard* when Ryan took the plate with a word of thanks and sauntered through to the sitting room as though he belonged here.

Which was—oh *God*, Sam had to stop his brain running ahead of itself as he thought how it would be if Ryan did belong here, if he came back with Sam every day after driving Bess and they talked about their days and Bess, and then ended up making out on the couch while the evening news was on the TV in the background.

Ryan had sat down on the couch, his thighs sprawling provocatively open. Sam saw the laptop sitting just inches away from him and swallowed hard as he remembered what he'd been watching when Ryan had knocked on the door. The way Ryan was sitting was an invitation for Sam to kneel between those open thighs and put to use some of what he'd been learning—mouthing at his cock through the softness of worn denim until Ryan was hard against his lips and moaning slightly, his hand threaded through Sam's hair as he pushed his crotch against Sam's mouth.

"You okay?"

Oh and *crap*, Sam was standing there with a plate in his hand, staring at Ryan's open thighs.

"Yeah," he croaked and, putting the laptop onto the floor, sat down next to Ryan. Because Ryan probably wasn't here for the same reason as last night, but Sam wasn't a complete idiot. He was going to make it as easy as possible, on the off-chance Ryan was interested.

He put his plate on his lap and hoped Ryan hadn't noticed the way his cock was trying to dig its way out of his jeans.

RYAN

Ryan hadn't thought this through. Story of his life, really—act first, think later. He'd sort of assumed he'd ask about his phone and they'd end up in Sam's bedroom looking for it. From there it was just the shortest of tumbles to the bed and by now they'd be having enthusiastic sex all over again.

Instead, he was sitting in a room that looked like it hadn't changed much from the 1960s, eating cheese on toast—which he hadn't had since his mum had left when he was five years old—and trying to figure out how this had happened. He wondered what his arrival had interrupted, and remembered again the way Sam had been pretty damn hard when he'd opened the door. Ryan knew he was sexy as fuck, but even the sight of *him* couldn't have got Sam going as quickly as that.

He nudged the laptop on the carpet with his toe. "You been talking to your fellow trainspotters?" he asked and tried to hide the smirk in his voice by stuffing more cheese on toast in his mouth. He knew damn well that wasn't what Sam had been doing.

Except—what if it was? What if he was some kind of fetishist that got off on trains? And then Ryan remembered the way Sam had been groaning under him last night and relaxed again. Sam might love Bessie, but he also loved cock.

He was also, predictably, bright red again. "Sort of," he said. "Hey, do you know why the Hereford train's such a mess at the moment?"

Ryan had to give the kid points for a gallant attempt at deflection. "No idea," he said firmly, biting into the other piece of his cheese on toast, and damn it was delicious. Cheddar so strong it could peel the paint off a wall—just the way he liked it. "I only do steam."

Sam's face fell, and Ryan felt bad.

"What do you mean by the train being a mess, anyway?" He could have kicked himself for encouraging the train conversation, but the way Sam perked up again somehow made up for it.

"All the carriages are out of order," he said. "It's been reverse formation for the past three weeks, and then yesterday it was completely jumbled up *and* it had a 47/7 loco, would you believe?"

"And that's noteworthy because...?"

"Because it's fitted with long-range fuel tanks and there's no way they're needed for that journey," Sam said. He grabbed his laptop and opened it. "Nobby says that when it passed through—*oh*."

If Ryan had thought he'd seen Sam blush before, he was very much mistaken. The kid looked like an overripe tomato that had been set on fire as he frantically hit buttons on the keyboard to mute the moaning and slapping flesh that echoed at disastrous volume from the laptop's speakers.

"Sounds like trainspotting's a whole lot more fun than I'd thought," Ryan said, putting his plate down and turning himself sideways on the sofa, an elbow propped on its back as he looked at Sam. "Tell me more."

Sam, his voice shaking, started to dive into an incomprehensible tangle of half-sentences about who the fuck knew what. Ryan watched him. The kid really was adorable. The kind some people would want to pet on the head and send home. But Ryan had seen his body, had felt just how much he loved being fucked, and he for one would be petting Sam somewhere other than his head later.

But fun though it would be just to move in a few inches and have the kid so turned around he didn't know what he was doing, until he simply gave in and opened his legs for Ryan, he didn't want to do that yet. Maybe he liked keeping them both on a knife-edge, which would make it all the more satisfying in the end. Or maybe he was actually enjoying sitting somewhere that felt like a home, listening to Sam, who was slowly getting his equilibrium back, talking about the *Mallard*. And that was a subject Ryan knew something about.

He took the offered laptop, first checking that Sam hadn't been wanking over it as he didn't want to get Sam's spunk on his fingers in any second-hand way, thank you very much—he had his own plans for just how and when he'd end up with Sam's spunk spattered on him—and looked at the diagram which Sam had opened on the screen, a schematic of the *Mallard's* double Kylchap blastpipe.

"Can you believe it, 126—well, 125.88—miles per hour," Sam said, and embarrassment was replaced by wonder in his voice.

Ryan nodded, because it was really bloody impressive, even allowing for the slight downward gradient of the track. "Yeah," he said. "Though I wouldn't have wanted to be in the cab just afterwards—"

"—when the aniseed stink bomb went off," Sam chorused with him.

Ryan had to fight not to batter his head against the back of the sofa when he realised anyone who'd heard them would think he was as much of a trainspotting nerd as Sam was. He wasn't. He was a Saunders. He was just taking a bit of a break from being a Saunders right now because it turned out this was fun, watching the dimples in Sam's cheeks when he grinned in utter joy about his favourite subject, and then glancing above the fireplace to see the not terribly good oil painting of the fastest steam locomotive ever built instead of some priceless piece of art that had been recommended by an interior designer.

Ryan stretched out on the sofa, something close to contentment filling him. "Any more cheese on toast?" he asked, and couldn't help his grin when Sam immediately scrambled to his feet and reached out for his plate. "Just remember, no Marmite," he warned, because Sam's piece had had that disgusting stuff swirled through the melted cheese until it was the colour of Bessie's smoke box after a particularly hard day.

He sat there, listening to Sam pottering about in the kitchen, and for the first time since he'd left this same house early that morning, he relaxed.

SAM

"I don't think Nobby likes me," Ryan complained, looking anything but upset as he passed the laptop back to Sam so he could see the forum's most prolific contributor appearing to suffer an apoplectic fit at the new member's latest post.

"I wonder why," Sam said. "Nothing to do with the fact you basically told him he doesn't know what he's talking about."

Ryan raised his eyebrows. "Let him prove it to me otherwise and I'll apologise."

Sam shouldn't be finding this so funny, because the guys on the forum were his *friends*, but Nobby had been too full of himself ever since he'd done that day-long driving experience course and was always quick to find fault with anyone who disagreed with him. It wouldn't do him any harm to be put in his place by someone with real experience.

"Oh, here we go," Ryan said, snatching back the laptop as it pinged. "Nope, he really doesn't like me. 'You, sir, are a troll and a vagabond'—a *vagabond*?" he asked Sam. "Is this guy for real? I think I'm going to stop posting before my fragile ego is shattered forever. Because apparently, *all* vacuum brakes in this country operated with the brake pipe at 21 Hg. You want to correct him on that?"

Sam, who would normally sink into a corner rather than challenge someone, even when he knew they were wrong, took the laptop back, signed in as himself—oldbess01—and proceeded to explain precisely why Nobby was wrong, linking him to GWR's archives to back himself up. It ended in Nobby flouncing from the forum, a couple of the other guys cheering Sam on and Ryan with a grin on his face the size of the *Mallard*'s driving wheels.

"I never knew trainspotting forums could be so much fun," he said, and immediately slapped himself in the forehead. "I didn't say that. And if you tell anyone I did, I'll tell everyone you were watching train porn when I got here."

The mention of sex reminded Sam all of a sudden that this was Ryan Saunders on his couch, and that their legs were touching. The first five minutes they'd been sitting there, he'd been so aware of Ryan's closeness and each breath he took that it felt like every nerve ending was on fire.

But then Ryan had decided he wanted to register for the forum so he could correct some of Nobby's more ridiculous claims, and as they'd passed the laptop back and forth between them, he'd managed to forget the fact that Ryan's shoulder was jostling his. Now all Sam could feel was the long line of Ryan's thigh pressed against his and the warmth of his bare arm brushing Sam's. His blood went south so fast he got lightheaded. Because, *damn*, how had he managed to spend the last hour messing about on train forums when he had Ryan Saunders sitting right next to him?

It seemed he wasn't the only one whose thoughts were turning that way. Ryan was leaning in, and Sam eagerly met him halfway, opening his lips beneath Ryan's mouth and welcoming his tongue, hungry and searching. He had just enough sense left to grab desperately at the laptop, which was making a bid for freedom, catching it as it slid off his lap and fumbling it onto the floor just before Ryan pressed him back on the couch until they were lying there, Ryan on top of him, touching all along their bodies, and most especially their hips.

And oh, *God*, this was better than *anything*—Ryan's hardening cock pushed against his. He rolled his hips up, and Ryan drew back, his eyes dark and his lips full, and then his mouth was against Sam's neck, nipping at the skin there.

"God, you're hungry for it, aren't you?" he said. His voice was rough and low, and maybe Sam should have felt ashamed because Ryan was making it sound like he was desperate or easy or something, but it was the truth. He wanted Ryan to kiss him, to touch him everywhere, to be inside him.

Sam's hands tangled in Ryan's T-shirt, tugging it up and over his head, Ryan helping him, and then there was all that warm skin and he was allowed to touch it. And he did. Over and over, fingers and hands sweeping over the long lines of his back, tracing the pattern of his ribs, and then, greatly daring, he slid a hand under the waistband of Ryan's jeans and stroked his firm, wonderful arse until Ryan was rutting against him, breathing heavily.

"If you don't stop that, we're not going to make it upstairs," he warned.

It was perhaps the only thing he could have said that would have got through to Sam. The speed with which he withdrew his hand had Ryan grinning, but not unkindly—it was a predatory look that made Sam want to rub against his cock all the more. But the thought of having all the space of his bed, of a repeat of last night, was even more tempting.

So when Ryan stood up, Sam didn't try to hold on to him but instead followed him up the steep flight of stairs in the corner of the room. And if he shocked himself with his bravery by reaching out to trail a hand over that gorgeous arse in those tight jeans, well, he only lived once and he reckoned he'd missed enough in his life already. He wasn't going to waste a single instant more. Not when he was about to have Ryan Saunders naked and in his bed again.

RYAN

Ryan's hands clenched the sheet beneath him as Sam knelt between his open legs, his head lowering so slowly to Ryan's cock that, if not for the look on Sam's face, Ryan would think he was the biggest fucking cocktease out there. But Sam's expression was a mixture of anticipation and deep thought, and he was looking at Ryan's cock with the same sort of delighted study he'd given to those schematics of the *Mallard*.

Anticipation or not, if he didn't fucking get on with it in the next three seconds—*fuck*. Ryan should be careful what he wished for because Sam's tongue dragged up his oh-so-ready cock like it was the best thing he'd ever tasted. Ryan's throaty groan seemed to encourage Sam, whose hands went to Ryan's hips to hold him steady as he started to conduct some sort of licking experiment, glancing up at Ryan's face each time he tried a new move, in a way that had Ryan caught between gasping at some of what Sam was doing and laughing helplessly. He'd never known anyone like Sam.

But finally, when Ryan was swearing with the need for more, Sam's mouth slid down on his cock, and it was hot and wet and just as good as his teasing had promised. His eyes stayed on Ryan's the whole time, as if to check he was doing this right. He hadn't taken Ryan in very far, but he was making up for that with his hand, not to mention enthusiasm.

A sound tore from Ryan's throat and he thrust his head back against the pillow, fighting for air, because Sam's long fingers were stroking his balls and it was fucking *amazing*. It was all he could do not to wind his hands into that hair and hold him steady and fuck his face. Except this was better than that, with Sam exploring, finding out what Ryan liked—and what he liked was Sam's mouth, moving like that, and if he didn't do something about this soon, it would be over before he knew it.

He forced his fingers away from where he'd been plucking at his nipples while Sam sucked his cock and wound a hand in Sam's hair, tugging him away.

Sam looked up at him, his lips wet and swollen, and his eyes dark and unsure.

"If you keep going like that, you're not going to get fucked for a while," Ryan said.

When he saw understanding, followed by hunger, chasing over Sam's face, he dragged him up the bed and rolled them over, so he was holding him down. Sam was breathing fast, excitement in his eyes and his cock hard against Ryan's.

"Is that what you want?" And fuck, Ryan didn't do bad porn dialogue. But somehow he got the feeling Sam liked being held like this, liked the way Ryan was levering Sam's legs apart, like Sam had no choice. "You want my cock inside you?"

"God, yes." Sam was trying to move, not to get away, but to arch up to give Ryan easier access.

Eventually Ryan let him move, and Sam promptly rolled over and got onto his knees to present his arse for Ryan to fuck. Ryan opened him up on his fingers and then pressed inside, Sam's moans muffled by the pillow his face was pressed into and his hands clenching reflexively around the wrought iron struts of the old-fashioned headboard. It felt so good that Ryan had to recite in his head every single one of Bessie's tolerance limits not to come too soon. Even that didn't help when Sam pushed back against him, demanding and eager, and Ryan forgot everything except the need to fuck Sam until he came, gasping Ryan's name, and Ryan tumbled over after him into orgasm.

This time he didn't even bother leaving the bed. He just got rid of the condom, tied it off and flung it in the direction of the bin. Anything more was beyond him. Though when Sam finally seemed to come to his senses and started pulling fretfully at the duvet beneath them, he moved enough to roll under it. He *knew* he shouldn't be doing this, but if he didn't get under the duvet first, Sam would steal all of the bed with his gigantic limbs and would have no compunction in defending his land-grab with knobbly knees and sharp elbows. So Ryan decided it was merely self-defence to get under there quickly. Once he'd recovered from coming that hard, he'd get his stuff together and get out.

That fucking alarm of Sam's was going to *kill* him. Ryan slumped back on the pillow from where he'd sat bolt upright in bed, heart racing as he blinked at the daylight coming through the curtains. Shit. He'd done it again—slept the whole night through. He couldn't remember doing that for years. Not sober, anyway.

He prodded Sam next to him and got a grumble in return as his hand was batted away. Sam really didn't do mornings.

"Good morning, sunshine," Ryan said, with an amount of fake enthusiasm that made even him want to hide under the duvet again.

"I hate you," Sam mumbled into his pillow, which of course was the invitation for Ryan to press in closer, letting Sam feel his very awake, very happy to see the morning cock, and nibble at the ticklish spot he'd found just where Sam's neck met the beginning of one of his gloriously broad shoulders.

Sam's grumbles turned into high-pitched giggles, and somehow it all ended up in a slow and easy handjob. Afterwards, looking at the blissful, dopey grin on Sam's face, Ryan thought it was a damn near perfect way to welcome the morning.

Chapter Seven

SAM

Sam was crunching the last of his Frosties when Ryan came out of the bathroom. He'd insisted on Sam going first. Sam had thought he was just being polite till he saw the way Ryan was hanging back at the far side of the kitchen when he emerged with Mabel in his hand. He knew some people were scared of spiders, but he couldn't believe Ryan Saunders was less than perfect. He was probably just...well, actually, there was no other explanation for what he was doing, edging backwards with every step forward that Sam took.

"He'll learn to like you," he'd promised Mabel as he set her down in the nasturtiums.

And then he'd crouched there, something in his chest tugging painfully as he realised what he was doing—assuming Ryan would be here long enough to get to know her. It had been two nights in a row, and somehow he'd started to think it would be every night from now on, and of course it wouldn't.

He still didn't know why Ryan had come round last night, but he did know it wasn't because they were starting some sort of relationship. That would involve dating and stuff. Whatever Val might think, he knew enough about the world to know this was just a hookup. The thought left him feeling a little sad.

But now, looking at Ryan's perfect body in that faded T-shirt and ripped jeans, looking like every one of Sam's teenage fantasies rolled into one, he couldn't hold on to that fleeting moment of sadness. This was so much more than he'd ever thought he could have.

"Do you want toast?" he asked.

Ryan shook his head, a rueful smile playing around his lips. "Is that your thing?" he asked. "Every time you see me, you try to feed me toast."

Well, that along with other things. And honestly, feeding Ryan toast wasn't top of Sam's list right now, with the bed waiting upstairs. He got up and put his bowl in the sink because otherwise Ryan would see the want on his face. And if he kept moving, he *wouldn't* say the words that were fighting to get out, just an innocent-sounding enquiry whether he'd see Ryan that night. He wanted to, so much, but he got the feeling Ryan wouldn't react well if he did. And why *should* he? It wasn't as if Sam had anything to offer.

He turned around from the sink to see Ryan making himself a coffee. As if he belonged here. Which, to Sam's mind, he did.

"What time do you need to be at work?" he asked, to stop anything else tumbling out of his mouth.

"Five minutes ago," Ryan said.

Sam gaped at him in horror. He didn't look the slightest bit worried, whereas Sam had never been late a day in his life and if this were him, he'd be racing down the street right now, fast as he could go, composing apology after apology to offer to Beaky when he got there. Ryan was merely concentrating on pouring water onto instant coffee in the *Mallard* mug.

He shrugged slightly. "It's not like they can fire me for being late," he said. Then his mouth twisted. "I mean, they can, but if I'm going to get sacked anyway, I might as well give them a reason."

"Sacked?" Sam stared at him, thinking he must have misheard. "Why on earth are you going to be sacked?"

"Because the trust that runs Bessie is in financial trouble. It's probably going to go bust if Cleaver is to be believed."

"But why would they sack *you* in that case? Surely that's the last expense they should cut, because the only way to get more money is to get more customers on Bess, and if she's not running, they can't do that." It didn't make any sense to Sam, and it was easier to think about that than face the unbearable thought that Bess might not run any more.

"My guess is they're going to get someone to replace me and pay them even less than they do me," Ryan said.

Sam was shaking his head. "No," he said, the force of his feeling poured into his voice. "That's not fair. They can't do that to you."

"Money talks," Ryan said. He set his barely touched coffee on the side. "I'm heading out," he said. "I'd offer you a lift, but I've only got one lid with me."

Sam was so busy thinking about whipping up Bess's passengers into some sort of protest that it took him a moment to realise what Ryan had said. And a few more to understand what he had meant, until he followed him into the hall and saw him pick up his motorcycle helmet.

"See you," Ryan said and pulled the door shut behind him.

Which left Sam having to lurk at the dining room window, hoping Ryan wouldn't spot him and think he was a creepy stalker as he watched Ryan swing his leg easily over the large, shiny motorbike parked outside the house. Something inside him twisted with how gorgeous Ryan looked, faded jeans with a rip in over his right knee showing a flash of skin, and denim stretched over the muscle of his thighs as he settled on the leather seat.

The roar of the bike starting up was so loud Sam was sure net curtains would be twitching up and down the street. Long after the sound had faded, Sam was still staring out at the empty spot where the bike had been parked. He couldn't understand how Ryan had just accepted that he'd be sacked. If it were him, he'd fight tooth and nail if someone wanted to take him away from Bess, and he was pretty sure Ryan felt the same way about her as he did.

Bess. If the trust was in that much trouble, Bess would have to be retired. He'd never again see her puffing her way into the station like she owned it or hear that haunting whistle echo around the valley as she steamed her way along the track. She'd been there his whole life, even when it seemed as if he'd lost everything else.

He didn't know what he'd do if he lost her as well.

RYAN

Ryan had needed to get out of there before Sam's logical thought processes led him to a question Ryan couldn't answer. Cleaver's threat to sack him was nonsensical to anyone who didn't know Ryan's father was *that* Saunders—the multimillionaire entrepreneur who turned up in the business pages of most newspapers at least once a week.

Cleaver had assumed that he could secure himself an income stream by threatening Ryan's job and had probably never thought he might have to make good on his threat. The thing was, Ryan knew the sort of man Cleaver was. Defiance would be punished with annihilation. Maybe he should introduce him to his father. Two of a kind like that would probably hit it off.

He opened the throttle gently when he got to the main road. He was careful these days about speed limits because he didn't want to have his fitness to drive Bessie called into question, but he could feel the bike under him just aching for him to open her up.

Part of him wanted to wind her up as fast as she'd go, head out of this dead-end town and leave everything behind. But a small part of him, a *stupid* part, still thought that perhaps there was a way he could keep driving Bessie and looking after her, and all the things that went with that which had him happier than he'd been in years. The problem was, there was no way he could fight Cleaver. He held all the cards, no matter how unfair Sam thought it was.

Warmth curled somewhere in Ryan's stomach as he remembered how indignant Sam had been, his dark hair flying as he'd shaken his head forcefully, protesting the injustice being done to Ryan. He couldn't remember the last time anyone had taken his side in anything, let alone with such natural, honest emotion. He didn't know how Sam had got to the age he had with his ideals still intact, but Ryan found himself hoping no one would shatter all that optimism.

He was getting to the point of being *seriously* late for work now and he'd got over his rebelliousness enough to realise how dumb it was to give Cleaver an excuse. Even so, as he pulled up outside his converted Georgian townhouse, he took a second to open the throttle one last gratuitous time just in case that snooty cow was still asleep, before racing up the stairs to his flat to change his clothes. When he headed out again, all thoughts of Sam Chancellor had been pushed to the back of his mind.

SAM

Melanie took Sam to one side just before lunch. "Is everything okay? You're at sixes and sevens again today."

He wanted to resent the way she—and the rest of them—mothered him, but he knew she meant it kindly. "Just got a few things on my mind," he said, and she nodded as if she understood and let him get back to unpacking bottles of baby lotion and putting them out on the shelf he'd just dusted.

He knew his mind had been on anything except work this morning, but unlike the previous day, he hadn't been daydreaming of Ryan Saunders naked. He'd been fighting the sick feeling deep in his stomach about Bess. And the thing was, he couldn't understand why the trust was in trouble. He knew it must be hellishly expensive to run her and the insurance must be through the roof, but during the school holidays and at weekends her carriages were always full. And it wasn't as if she was struggling for passengers during the week, with the steam enthusiasts who came from miles away to ride on her and all the pensioners who took advantage of the OAP discount.

He stared at the bottle he'd been holding for the last five minutes and wondered what he was supposed to be doing with it. Oh, that was right—put it out on the shelf.

Old Bess had nearly been mothballed back in the '80s because all the new health and safety legislation had been too much for the then trustees, who'd been a bunch of enthusiastic amateurs who just wanted to keep her running. But then the local paper had run a story about the threat to her on the front page every day for a week, because the editor, whose daughter Dawn worked in the pharmacy with Sam, was a huge fan of Bess. Some local businesspeople had stepped up and volunteered to be trustees.

Ever since then, there'd been no suggestion of financial difficulties. The ticket prices had gone up every year, but then, show him something that hadn't. Uncle Ken had been close friends with one of the trustees, Mr Johnson, who had died in January, and there'd never been so much as a whisper that the trust was finding it hard to make ends meet.

And it *still* didn't make sense that they'd want to replace Ryan as the driver as their first step to try and cut costs. People who paid peanuts got monkeys, as Uncle Ken used to say, and this was one job that had to be done right—one mistake could blow that boiler apart, taking a hell of a lot of people with it.

Sam frowned. The only thing that'd changed in recent years had been the appointment of that bloke Cleaver as Chief Operating Officer three or four years ago. He remembered Uncle Ken saying there'd been some disagreement among the trustees over his appointment, but to be honest, he hadn't paid much attention at the time.

He wished now that he had. He wished Mr Johnson was still alive so he could ask him directly—and then he realised that unless Mrs Johnson had got rid of all her husband's paperwork, she'd still have everything that had gone to the trustees, including the accounts.

Several years ago, Sam had spent many happy days in the Johnsons' sun-filled dining room, papers from the trust spread all over the table as he'd burrowed out facts for a project he was writing on Bess for school. Maybe those accounts would show him what had gone wrong. Maybe there *wasn't* any financial trouble, but Cleaver just wanted to get rid of Ryan and this was an excuse. And if that was the case and they could prove it from the accounts, then surely the unions or employment tribunals or something would get involved and Ryan would keep his job.

His hands were trembling slightly as he put the rest of the bottles out as quickly as he could go. Then he went to see Melanie, to ask if he could take an early lunch. The sooner he could phone Mrs Johnson, the sooner he'd find out if she still had the papers that could solve all their problems.

RYAN

Ryan stepped out of the staffroom into the evening sunshine. His overalls were in a bag at his side because they *really* needed washing. He'd surprised himself by enjoying all the physical labour that was necessary to keep Bessie in driving order, but the one thing he hadn't got used to was the dirt, with grease and oil finding their way even through his overalls. And then there was the charming daily task of cleaning her ash pan. The first thing he did when he got home every day was take a long, hot shower, and today in particular he couldn't wait, because the sun had been fierce for May.

The good weather had brought the crowds out, and he'd done a quick calculation as he'd watched the passengers queuing to get onto the carriages. Running an engine like Bessie was expensive, but they also made a lot of money every day in ticket sales. And then there was the little shop which sold mass-produced crap with Bess's likeness printed on—though he probably shouldn't say too much about it being crap given he wore one of the shop's engine driver caps to keep the sun out of his eyes. Marlene, the lady who ran the shop, had given it to him for free when she'd seen him squinting into the sun. Hell, if Cleaver heard about that, it would probably be a sacking offence all on its own—accepting stolen goods or something like that.

He kicked the staffroom door behind him, just to make sure it was properly shut, not because of the anger that swirled through him at the thought of that bastard.

"Ryan!"

The slightly breathless call echoed along the empty platform, and he looked up to see Sam hurtling down the footbridge steps towards him. The sight of Sam lifted Ryan's spirits, right up until he saw the excitement and pleasure on Sam's face, and then his heart sank. Oh, God, that was all he needed. Ryan felt like the biggest prick alive, but he was going to have to tell the kid to sod off. To explain to him that it had just been sex between them.

"I need to talk to you." Sam's gaze darted around the platform as he spoke. "But not here."

Ryan was still wondering how to get rid of him kindly when he leaned in and said close against Ryan's ear, "I don't want to risk anyone else hearing this."

It had Ryan's stomach plummeting as he looked for an escape. But the only way out of the station was across the footbridge and then through the long corridor. He could just tell Sam here and now it was over, but he'd obviously got soft in his old age because he wanted to let the kid down gently, not least because Sam was practically vibrating with excitement at the prospect of telling Ryan he loved him.

Ryan had his hands jammed in his jeans pockets when they reached the exit to the station, trying to pull himself together enough to say in a way that wouldn't crush the kid forever that Ryan wasn't interested in anything other than a quick fuck.

That was when Sam leaned close again and informed him in a thrilled whisper that he'd got access to the financial records of the trust that looked after Old Bess.

It took Ryan a moment to change gears. But then he stared at Sam blankly, unable to follow the significance of this statement. "So what?"

It stopped Sam in his tracks. The excitement in his eyes vanished and his whole body seemed to close down, until he looked like the guy Ryan had first met—anxious and self-conscious.

"I mean, why do you think that would help?" he asked, trying to soften it. His first question still stood, but he hated the way it had made Sam look.

"I just—I guess—I mean, I thought that if we could prove there *aren't* financial problems, it would mean that the threat to fire you was personal." Sam stumbled over the words. "And once people know that, he wouldn't be able to get away with it and your job would be safe."

The threat was pretty fucking personal all right, though not for the reasons Sam assumed. He doubtless thought Ryan had pissed off the wrong person. Ryan knew better. All Cleaver wanted was to get as much money for the trust as possible. That way he could build a wildly successful empire out of a sleepy little charity and would be snapped up by a high-profile, high-paying company for a senior management position.

It was a pattern he'd seen too many times to count. The difference with Cleaver was that he wasn't bright enough to be subtle about it, and he'd pushed too fast, rather than letting Ryan stew for long enough to change his mind.

He frowned slightly, remembering how desperate Cleaver had seemed when he'd given Ryan that ultimatum. There'd been sweat on his temples, and however good an actor Cleaver might be, Ryan didn't think he could have caused that on purpose. Maybe he really *had* been desperate. Maybe Cleaver had fucked up the running of the railway and was actually looking for a way out of a financial hole before the trustees found out and sacked him. All Ryan would have to do would be to let Cleaver know that he knew, with the unspoken understanding that as long as Ryan kept his job, he wouldn't tell anyone else. It wouldn't be blackmail. It would be survival.

"I mean, isn't it worth at least having a look?" Sam asked, sounding unsure yet determined. "Mrs Johnson has got all the minutes and reports and accounts from 1986 onwards."

Ryan nodded. He guessed he couldn't see what harm it could do. As he saw the delight dawn in Sam's eyes at his agreement, he realised—the kid had done this for him. He wasn't fooling himself that keeping Bess running hadn't been on Sam's mind as well, but what had spilled out of his mouth had been about Ryan's job. That unaccustomed warmth flickered inside him again.

"She's said we can go round at half-past seven tonight if we want," Sam said. "I wasn't sure—I mean, I didn't know if you might have other plans..." He trailed off uncertainly.

"Nothing that can't be cancelled," Ryan said. The evening that had lain ahead of him involved a shower, a meal and then finding ways to fill the time until heading to bed, where he probably wouldn't be able to sleep until the early hours anyway.

Sam looked a little crushed, and before he knew he was going to, Ryan found himself adding, "I'm sure the microwave meal and sofa won't hold it against me."

Sam's grin rivalled the sun for brightness. Ryan had the feeling that he shouldn't be encouraging Sam this way, but decided to ignore those thoughts because there was something mildly addictive about that smile. Instead, he concentrated on arranging to meet Sam later.

SAM

Sam had quailed slightly when Mrs Johnson had shown them into the dining room, because there were *stacks* of full ring binders on the table. "I'm not sure which ones you're interested in this time, Sam dear," she said, "so I got all of them ready for you."

She'd actually said a whole lot more than that, to the point where Sam was pretty sure Ryan was close to leaving because at this rate they were never going to get to the paperwork even if they were gaining an encyclopaedic knowledge of how the late Mr Johnson had come to be one of the trustees. But then a phone had rung somewhere in the house, and with an apologetic smile she'd retreated to take the call.

"Where do we start?" Sam asked.

"The most recent set of accounts," Ryan said, pulling the closest stack of files to him and starting to look through them. "Yeah, these are last year's. We might not know the real costs of running Bessie, but if we compare the accounts over a number of years, it should give us an idea whether patterns have changed recently."

Sam nodded and pulled his notepad and pen out of his satchel. Ryan's face had been a picture when he'd seen Sam pick it up to bring with him, but it was the only thing he had that was big enough to carry an A4 notepad for the notes he expected to make.

Sam's first look at the paperwork had him wondering if he'd done something really stupid by suggesting this. The accounts ran into pages upon pages, with entries full of nonsense words like "amortisation" and "accruals". Ryan, though, had his lips pursed as he skimmed the pages thoughtfully and looked like he actually understood them.

"Interesting," he said at last, and sat back. "You want to take photos of all the pages so we've got them to go through in detail later? If we try to analyse them now, we'll still be here this time next year. And that, I think, is the point."

Sam looked up from where he was getting his phone out so he could take the pictures Ryan wanted. "Sorry?"

"Anyone who reads these is going to end up drowned in detail. Maybe it's the law for a trust, but if anyone presented these sorts of accounts to any firm's AGM, they'd be booted out so fast their head would spin. Annual accounts are all that's expected and needed, not so much detail it makes you give up the will to live, let alone want to read it to the end."

Sam wanted to ask Ryan how he knew so much about business accounts, but Ryan was already pulling another folder towards him, so instead he concentrated on taking photos.

An hour later, Ryan was deep in paperwork, chewing on Sam's pen, which he'd picked up at some point to make incomprehensible scribbles on Sam's notepad. Sam felt like a spare part. He couldn't make head or tail of all the information. But at least he could watch Ryan, seeing the slight crease between his eyes and the focus in his face as he read through the pages before him. Not to mention those full lips sucking on his pen in a way that was giving Sam all sorts of ideas about how those same lips would look wrapped around his cock, those long dark eyelashes lowered in the way they were right now as he concentrated on the figures before him, except in Sam's version his hazel eyes would then look up, warm and teasing as Ryan's mouth slid down on him.

He jumped when the door opened and Mrs Johnson came in, carrying a tea tray. He got up and swiftly cleared a space on the table—her neat piles of folders had long ago been transformed into a disordered mess—and prayed she couldn't see a trace of what he'd just been thinking in his face.

"I hope you're finding what you need," she said. "I know Andrew was always very careful about keeping absolutely everything because, as he said, you never could tell where a lawsuit might come from. He printed out every email he got that was to do with the trust and filed those as well, of course. It's a wonder anyone volunteers to be a trustee of anything these days, really, with all the rules and regulations. I don't know how anyone gets anything *done* by the time all the forms are filled out, and it's all done over the Internet these days, of course, which isn't very sensible as most people who are trustees are older people with time on their hands, and of course they're not going to be very good at using computers. Milk or lemon, Ryan?"

Her presence put paid to any reading for the next five minutes, but she *finally* retreated, still talking until the door closed behind her, leaving Ryan and Sam in blessed silence. Ryan shook his head. "How did her husband cope?"

"Why do you think he was on so many committees, if not to get out of the house?" Sam asked. As Ryan's teeth flashed in a quick grin he felt bad for poking fun at Mrs Johnson. "She's a good person," he said. "She just likes to talk, I guess."

"No shit, Sherlock," Ryan murmured, reaching out to the gold-rimmed porcelain plate which sported an array of homemade biscuits. His eyelids fluttered as he bit into the macaroon he selected, and he made a little moan that had Sam half-hard within seconds because *God*, what he'd give to hear Ryan moan like that in bed. What he'd give to be the one who *made* Ryan moan like that.

"I take it back," Ryan said, gazing at the macaroon in lustful adoration. "If she can bake like this, she can talk all she wants."

Sam snagged one of two shortbread fingers that Ryan's removal of the macaroon had revealed. If he scoffed it quickly enough, he'd get to the other one before Ryan realised that, good as Mrs Johnson's macaroons were, her shortbread was worth killing over.

The second shortbread went down almost as fast as the first, so that by the time Ryan finally finished chewing, a dreamy look on his face that wasn't helping the state of Sam's cock in the least, there was no evidence left of Sam's pre-emptive raid on the biscuit plate. He plastered an innocent look on his face as he wiped his hands on his jeans and picked up his phone again, but from the narrowing of Ryan's eyes, he suspected it might not have worked.

RYAN

Truth to tell, Ryan was glad of Mrs Johnson's interruption. His head was swimming from looking through so many badly presented sets of accounts. It was a little disturbing how many of his father's lessons came back to him as he looked for patterns rather than allowing himself to be drowned in the details.

And there were so many details, right down to the lists of consumables for Bessie's upkeep—and holy *shit*, did a brake compressor really cost that much? He wondered just what qualifications or experience someone needed to become a member of the board of trustees, because anyone unused to reading business accounts for a living would be likely to end up looking at the bolded lines that gave the totals for each section and imagine they'd grasped what was going on. He thought about asking Mrs Johnson what her husband's job had been before he'd become a trustee, but swiftly decided he didn't have the stamina to cope with the answer.

He began to concentrate on the minutes of the AGM four years ago, before Cleaver was appointed, and those from three years ago, when he was in post. Ryan expected that whatever they were looking for would be found in the accounts, but if Cleaver was trying to handwave away his incompetence, there might also be some clue in the record of the meetings. His father had always said that anyone trying to hide something couldn't stop themselves leaving some sort of sign pointing to it—either their conscience trying to make up for what they were doing or their ego unable to resist displaying how clever they were. He'd get Sam to take photos of the minutes as well.

Looking at Sam, he noticed a small row of sugar crystals just above his lip that he seemed completely unaware of as he snapped photo after photo. Probably from those biscuits he'd guzzled down so fast. Ryan had noticed the covetous looks Sam had cast at the plate while eating the first one so quickly he'd practically inhaled it. Apparently, sweet, polite Sam disappeared when it came to important things like food, or how much of the bed he got to sleep in.

Remembering how Sam's attempt at claiming the whole bed last night had ended up in Ryan putting him firmly in his place—which just happened to be on his back and under him—had Ryan leaning forward and swiping those sugar crystals away with the pad of his thumb.

Sam's hands clenched on his phone and he stared at Ryan, looking shocked, his lips very slightly apart as he drew in a sharp breath. Which of course led Ryan to run his thumb along that lower lip, feeling its soft plumpness for himself. He didn't expect Sam's tongue to flick out and lick his thumb.

Heat pooled in Ryan's groin. And when Sam pushed his mouth slowly onto his finger, warm and slick, tongue playing against it before he abandoned all finesse and simply sucked, Ryan was hard as hell. God, he wanted Sam on his knees, sucking his cock with just that much enthusiasm.

But he just *knew* if he gave in to temptation, Mrs Johnson would walk back in and though she'd probably be talking too much to even notice Sam giving him a blowjob right in front of her, Sam would never recover from the shame. So instead he settled for sliding his hand into that dark messy hair and encouraging Sam's mouth off his finger so that when Sam looked at him, startled and a little anxious, he could cover those lips with his own. Could show Sam just how talented *his* tongue could be in return.

As they kissed, as Sam opened his mouth further and started making little noises into Ryan's mouth, Ryan's hand found its way to Sam's crotch. The hard length of his cock felt fucking good through the denim as he stroked it, and Sam's hips pushed upwards into his touch, needing more.

The phone rang in the silent house, startling them both and causing Ryan to pull back. Sam's eyes were dark, his lips wet and open, and *God*, if that damned woman would answer that damned phone, Ryan was sure they'd have enough time for something more because she wouldn't let even a wrong number go without talking the person at the other end to death.

But as his breath started coming more easily, he realised that was stupid. They needed to get this information, and they'd have the whole night ahead of them once they were out of this place. Then he would show Sam exactly what he could do with his tongue when he put his mind to it.

He wrenched his mind back to balance sheets. And if it took Sam a few moments longer to stop staring at him and pick up his phone again, well, Ryan was only human. No one could blame him for feeling a little smug.

SAM

It was only five minutes' walk to his house from Mrs Johnson's, but it felt like five miles because the whole way Sam was agonising over how to ask Ryan if he wanted to come in. He guessed asking him in for coffee was too obvious. Asking him in for sex had the benefit of being straightforward and accurate, but despite Sam's shamelessness earlier—and he still couldn't believe he'd *done* that with Ryan's finger—he couldn't be that blatant. What if Ryan fixed him with a withering stare and laughed at him? It wasn't as if they'd have seen each other tonight if not for the trust records.

It turned out Sam was overthinking things, just for a change. Instead of getting on his bike and leaving when they got back to the house, Ryan followed him to the front door without even being asked, and then stared in bemusement at the plastic container on the doorstep. "Why's there a box of weeds outside your door?"

Sam scooped up the box and wondered just how amazed, on a scale of stunned to flabbergasted, his visitor had been not to find him at home in the evening. "Spinach, not weeds," he said, once he got a look at the contents of the ice cream tub.

"Not exactly answering my question."

"The Garden Club," Sam said, unlocking the front door. "They're like the Cardale Mafia."

Ryan followed him in. "I'm no expert, but I don't think the Mafia's known for leaving boxes of spinach outside people's houses," he said, shrugging off his jacket and hanging it on the hook.

"Not that," Sam said, trying not to smile too broadly at the realisation he hadn't had to say anything to get Ryan to stay. "I mean the way they know everyone and everything in the town."

"So if you don't pay your protection money, you get spinach on your doorstep? Sounds pretty harsh to me."

But for all Ryan's questioning, he didn't seem that interested in the answer. The spinach ended up all over the carpet as he pushed Sam against the wall, his mouth on Sam's in a deep kiss and his hands roaming.

Sam had gone from nought to ninety in two seconds—he was kissing Ryan back, hard and deep as he moved against him. They were both wearing far too many clothes for this. And when Ryan pulled Sam's T-shirt off, Sam did everything he could to help, right up until the instant Ryan's mouth closed around his nipple, tongue flicking at it and teeth tugging, and Sam whimpered.

"Bed," he got out, and scarcely recognised his own voice.

It looked almost as if Ryan wasn't going to bother with moving, and *God*, just the thought of Ryan turning him around and taking him against the wall was unbelievably hot, except he wanted to touch Ryan as much as he wanted Ryan to be inside him. He breathed in a shuddering gasp as Ryan finally pulled back, took his wrist in a strong grip and tugged him up the stairs.

Sam still wanted to touch Ryan, to explore every part of his body with his hands and his mouth, to see if he could wring from him the same moan of pure pleasure that the damn macaroon had managed, but Ryan was making that impossible. Somehow Sam had ended up in the middle of the bed on his back, his knees spread wide as Ryan finger-fucked him, blunt, thick fingers moving in and out in a way that had Sam moaning. And then his large cock was pressing in.

Sam loved everything Ryan did to him, but it turned out that being fucked was the holy grail for him, having his arse filled with Ryan's hot, hard cock, having it thrusting into him until he lost his mind and the world whited out as he came.

After Ryan had finished, he was the one who got them under the covers because Sam didn't think he'd be able to move again, boneless, drowsy and utterly content. He wrapped an arm around Ryan and moved close against him, and only when Ryan stiffened slightly did he think maybe he shouldn't have done that. But as he thought about pulling back, Ryan relaxed, and it was beginning to feel so right sharing the bed with someone, no longer being alone in an empty house, that Sam fell asleep nearly straightaway.

It seemed like only minutes later that he woke up with a jerk as his alarm went off. In some sort of desperate hope Ryan might come back with him, Sam had not only changed his sheets before heading to Mrs Johnson's but had optimistically set his alarm half an hour earlier than usual. Something he was now deeply regretting as he hit out blindly in its direction, hoping to find the snooze button.

"You really are rubbish at mornings." Ryan's voice in his ear was deep and a little hoarse with sleep, but also amused.

Sam muttered something—he had no idea what, but even at this ungodly hour his manners were too deeply ingrained simply to ignore the freakish morning person lying next to him. As Ryan threw the covers back and got out of bed, he made a futile grab for them, intending to pull them back over himself and get at least five minutes more sleep.

"No way," Ryan informed him, brutally yanking the quilt off the bed entirely before scouting about the room and picking up his clothes from the previous night, and how had his T-shirt ended up on the bookcase? Sam had a vague memory of being so desperate to touch him that clothes had become the enemy, to be pulled off and got rid of as quickly as possible. "You need to get up and deal with Shelob so I can shower."

"Her name's Mabel," Sam muttered sulkily, staying precisely where he was. It didn't do him much good because Ryan pulled back the curtains, flooding the room with daylight. "Oh for God's *sake*," Sam whimpered, burying his head under his pillow.

"Up," Ryan said, then paused.

The length of the following silence had Sam emerging from the safety of his pillow to find out what was going on. Ryan was unabashedly surveying Sam's naked body as he lay curled up in his last-ditch attempt to continue happily snoozing.

"Well, that particular command might be redundant," he said, his eyes on Sam's usual morning wood. Sam really wasn't awake enough to understand how things went in the space of a minute from Ryan doing the best drill sergeant impression he'd ever seen to waking Sam up properly, with a long, languorous and best *ever* blowjob.

By the time they were done, Sam was more than happy to go and rescue Mabel, before having the quickest of showers himself and making tea and toast, ready for when Ryan emerged from the shower. As he spread Marmite on his toast, making sure the jar didn't get close enough to contaminate Ryan's toast by proximity, he thought this was the way mornings should always be.

Chapter Eight

SAM

When Mrs Johnson pushed open the dining room door, using her elbow because she was carrying a laden tea tray, Ryan shot out of his seat and held the door for her, earning an enchanted, girlish look up into his face. Sam guessed even age was no defence against the deadly weapon of Ryan's smile.

"Thank you, dear," she said as she put the tray on the table and proceeded to pour them each a cup of tea. "I hope you don't mind fending for yourselves for the rest of the evening. I've got the girls coming round to play bridge."

Murmuring a polite response, Ryan took his seat again, gallantly passing the first teacup and then a plate over to Sam. He took both, a trifle surprised at Ryan's solicitousness. All became clear, however, when Ryan took his own tea from Mrs Johnson with a smile that would have melted the hardest heart, and she offered him the biscuit plate first.

Sam stared, utterly betrayed, as Ryan snagged the single shortbread finger that had nestled among the chocolate buns. He somehow managed not to say anything until Mrs Johnson was gone again, door firmly closed behind her, and then he turned on Ryan.

"You *sod*."

Ryan grinned back, looking disgustingly smug and pleased with himself. "Yep," he said with satisfaction, and sank his teeth into the crumbly goodness of the best shortbread in the history of the world.

Sam stared forlornly at his plate. The chocolate bun he'd taken in order to be polite just didn't match up against Mrs Johnson's shortbread. Ryan sighed, leaned over, and put what was left of the shortbread on it.

"You look like I murdered your puppy," he said. "For God's sake, you have it."

It wasn't as if Sam fell in love with Ryan Saunders because of a piece of shortbread, but in that moment he realised that as well as being hotter than hell, amazing in bed and a freaking *engine driver*, Ryan was kinder than he'd ever let anyone guess. Sam's heart turned over in his chest, and there was a lump in his throat. It didn't, however, stop him from cramming the shortbread in his mouth as fast as he could go, because he wasn't going to risk Ryan changing his mind.

"Thanks," he said, through a mouthful of crumbs.

Apart from the occasional bursts of laughter that floated across the hall from the sitting room—something to do with the bottle of wine that had been laid out on the green baize table alongside the packs of cards, Sam thought—they were undisturbed for the rest of the evening and managed to photograph every last scrap of paper that Ryan wanted. After thanking Mrs Johnson by poking their heads into the sitting room where four elderly ladies sat, grimly intent on the cards in their hands, they walked home together.

The problem was, Sam thought, glancing sideways at Ryan, that he could really get used to this, to spending every evening and night with Ryan. But while he might not have any experience of relationships, he knew enough to know that whatever was going on between them wasn't a relationship. Ryan hadn't wanted a date—he'd just wanted sex that first time.

And it wasn't like they talked about feelings or the future, or anything that wasn't to do with trains. It was just that the more time Sam spent with Ryan, the more he wanted to spend time with him. To get to know him better and to understand what made him seem so arrogant in some ways, yet underneath it be kind and thoughtful.

When they reached Sam's house and Ryan came in with him again, and they had sex and crawled under the covers together again, he felt a fragile hope growing inside him that possibly this had turned into more than just blowing off steam. And then he snorted into his pillow, which earned him an elbow in the ribs from an annoyed Ryan who'd nearly been asleep, because however frighteningly perfect Ryan Saunders might seem, if he used a line like that he was really just as much a dork as Sam.

On that comforting thought, he fell asleep.

RYAN

Leaving work the next evening, Ryan found Sam had already emailed him the photos he'd taken. Over a disgusting supermarket ready meal that claimed to be beef stroganoff but tasted like rubberised cat shit, he started to go through them, printing out the pages that seemed of interest so that he could easily compare them side by side.

His feeling that something didn't add up with these accounts intensified as he combed through them. The expenditure on Bessie's upkeep had gone up exponentially three years ago and had remained at that level ever since. He knew that some maintenance tests only needed doing every few years, and then there were the things that only needed checking every five years, like staybolt caps and sleeves, and of course different parts of her wore out at different rates so there was never going to be a completely steady figure, but the outgoings had remained sky-high. According to the minutes, Cleaver had explained it to the trustees by talking about her increasing age and new safety regulations being more demanding, and Ryan knew that it was all hand-waving *bollocks*.

He got up to make a cup of tea. He'd been hunched over for hours studying this stuff, and he was stiff. It was a shame Sam wasn't there to give him a massage, because Sam had gone from being uncertain and slightly grabby with those huge hands of his to getting to know just how and where Ryan liked to be touched. And right now the thought of him working the aches out of his shoulders before turning his attentions elsewhere sounded pretty damn good.

He made himself some tea and stood at the window, gazing out over the marketplace below. It must be later than he'd realised because the pubs were closed, and even the teenage kids who hung around the war memorial were gone. Glancing at his watch, he found it was nearly two in the morning. *Hell*, he was going to regret this tomorrow. He should go to bed now. But he knew there was something there, tantalising him, just out of his reach. It was as if he could see it from the corner of his eye, but when he turned to look at it, he lost it. He'd give it another half hour and see if he could find what it was he was missing.

Fifty minutes later, he had it. It was so blindingly obvious he couldn't believe he'd missed it, but then, he'd been looking for incompetence, not *fraud*.

One of the previous year's expenditure line items was a new Johnson bar. Nothing wrong with that, except for the small fact that as someone who touched that lever every single day, he knew damn well it wasn't new. Once he'd realized that, he found claims for all sorts of bits and pieces for Bessie from the same supplier, totalling thousands upon thousands of pounds, and *none of them were in use*. Not one. As he dug further, he found that particular supplier had been listed in the accounts for the first time three years ago.

Holy *fuck*. Someone was defrauding the trust on a huge scale, and no one had spotted it. But now that he had, it was just like his father had always said—whoever was responsible for this had put the noose around their own neck. They thought they'd been clever in providing so much detail that no one would ever plough through it and discover the discrepancies, but by listing it all out, item by item, they'd put the evidence out there for anyone who knew Bessie. He guessed that the people with that level of knowledge of Bessie were exceedingly thin on the ground, and none of those would normally have any interest in reading the accounts.

Tiredness disappeared under a surge of triumph at his accomplishment. For about thirty seconds, right up until he realized that he didn't know what to do next. He was pretty sure it was Cleaver who was responsible—not just because he was a dick, though if Ryan was honest that was part of his reasoning, but because he didn't see who else could have done it. Cleaver had defended the expenditure to the board; that meant he must have studied the accounts beforehand and even *he* would have picked up that they were several thousand pounds adrift from where they should be year after year.

But who the hell could Ryan tell? The police? He snorted. Yeah, right. Like they'd believe *him*. If he told the trustee board and any of them were in on it, he was stuffed. If he told them and they *weren't* in on it, they still weren't going to believe some minion who was about to be sacked versus the man they'd chosen to run the business, whose lies they'd bought hook, line and sinker for the past three years.

He was fucked. There was no one he could go to with this and Cleaver was going to sack him. He might as well face that fact. But unlike everything else in his life, this wasn't his fault, and it wasn't *fair*.

He finally went to bed but was still staring at the ceiling when his alarm went. Switching it off, he sighed. He might as well quit now and not give Cleaver the satisfaction of firing him. But something inside him refused to give up. If today was the last time he'd drive Bessie, he'd enjoy it. Even if this was all coming to an end, at least he'd had the chance to experience something few other people ever did.

As he headed out of his flat, careful to slam the door behind him to make sure the cow in the flat next to him got woken up, that knowledge was very little comfort.

SAM

Sam had spent a frustrating evening poring over the papers that Ryan had asked him to photograph. He just couldn't understand them. It didn't stop him trying, though—they had to save Ryan's job, and they had to save Bess. And he tried to pretend that no part of his motivation was the selfish one of keeping Ryan in Cardale.

After a restless night—because apparently he'd become so used to sharing the bed with someone that it had felt wrong without Ryan there beside him, muttering peevishly about Sam being a blanket hog whenever they wrestled over the quilt—he headed to work. His mind wasn't on whatever joys awaited him today at the shop, but instead on trying to make sense of what he'd read the night before. He'd been so sure that if they could look at the accounts, they could prove the trust wasn't in trouble and that Cleaver was just trying to get rid of Ryan. He hadn't expected them to be so difficult to understand, let alone for them to go into excruciating detail like...

Bloody hell.

He stopped dead in the middle of the pavement and reached into his pocket for his phone. When he flicked to the photos of Bess he'd taken on the rainy day she'd puffed proudly into the station with two newly restored carriages added to the length of the train she pulled, the date bore out his memory.

It had been almost precisely two years ago, and he knew that the capacity of the new carriages was approximately 34% greater than the smaller, older ones that had been her companions all these years. But the notes to the part of the accounts that dealt with revenue from tickets sales didn't reflect that. Where her occupancy ratio was recorded, it was based on the same number of seats for every carriage. It might be only a few hundred ticket sales adrift per week, but over the whole season that racked up to thousands of pounds.

He stared at the photo of Bess, not quite able to believe the leaps his mind was making. Because if he was right—and he *knew* he was—then whatever lies Cleaver was telling Ryan were almost irrelevant against the fact that someone was ripping off the trust. Damn it, he *had* to tell Ryan.

But he could see the bus coming, and if he missed this one, he'd be late for work. Anyway, Ryan would be in the engine shed now, so Sam wouldn't be able to see him, and Cleaver didn't let him and Simon have their phones on them during the day in case they were tempted to use them for personal calls. He was a bit of a git that way, Sam thought, as he ran for the bus. Sam would just have to go and see Ryan tonight after work, even if he felt as if he'd burst, having to wait until then.

As he showed the bus driver his pass and made his way to a seat, he realised—this way, they'd probably spend the evening together again. And possibly the night. Yes, it was definitely worth waiting. It wasn't as if giving this information to Ryan a few hours earlier would change anything, after all.

RYAN

It was just as well Bessie was a sweet-tempered old lady, Ryan thought as he finished the maintenance on her that evening. She'd been forgiving about the fact he hadn't had his full attention on her at all times. Her wheels had slipped once, very briefly, and he'd been aware of Simon's gaze because it wasn't like Ryan to allow that, but he hadn't said anything.

Just as well, because Simon might just have got a sharp answer as the day wore on and Ryan's temper, fuelled by his tiredness, grew like the fire in Bessie's belly. Someone—and his money was most definitely on Cleaver—was helping themselves to something that wasn't theirs, and while he couldn't exactly take the moral high ground given his past, the end result was that he was left with the choice of crawling to his father or losing his job, all because someone couldn't keep their sticky fingers out of the till.

Simon was long gone by the time Ryan finished. He didn't blame him. Hives of bees were probably more pleasant company than he was right now. He locked Bessie's shed and headed off to the staffroom, where he could get out of the overalls that were too damn hot in this weather. He wasn't sure whether he was relieved or slightly disappointed when he got to the platform and there was no Sam there waiting for him. Relieved, he told himself, because right now he needed some time on his own to open up his bike on the long curves of the hills around the town and regain his equilibrium.

He had the feeling that if he let his temper out by snarling at Sam, Sam would neither come back at him nor shrug it off. Those eyes of his would grow dark and hurt and make Ryan feel bad. Ryan didn't have the patience for that tonight. The very fact he'd sort of expected Sam to be there and he wasn't fed his temper. God damn it, he was a Saunders and he didn't need anyone. He certainly didn't need to hang out with some trainspotting nerd.

He strode over the footbridge and through the station, his leather jacket over his shoulder. All the other staff had long gone, living the small town life where everything shut at 6 p.m., though there was a trickle of commuters who were heading the other way for him to navigate. For the first time since he'd started here, this felt like a job.

The irony that it only did so because it was about to be taken away wasn't lost on him as he started up the steep stone steps to the staff car park. He dug in his pocket for his keys, the edges of the pewter key ring that Marlene had pressed on him digging into his hand. He was trying to avoid Marlene now, because the frequency with which she gave him stuff meant he was going to end up with the entire crappy stock of the shop in his flat. At least the key ring was useful, though as it was in the shape of a steam engine he'd have to make sure no one else ever saw it. It was the sort of thing Sam would own and proudly use.

Some bloke in a hoodie—in this weather, seriously?—started down the steps just as Ryan got halfway up them. Fucking typical. There was hardly room to pass and this dickhead couldn't wait thirty seconds? He wasn't even moving to the side but kept coming down the centre of the steps, right in Ryan's way.

"Look, mate," Ryan said.

That was as far as he got. A fist slammed into his face, snapping his head back. He clutched blindly at the handrail for balance, but a hard shove to his chest had him falling backwards. He went down like a fucking bowling pin, the impact driving the breath from his body as he hit the step behind him and kept going.

Chapter Nine

SAM

Beaky had been in a vile mood for some reason. "His wife," Melanie had said to Dawn earlier, when Sam had been in hearing distance, but he had no idea how she could know that. So he kept his head down and did his job. It included a stint of filling in behind the pharmacy counter, which he *hated* because he hadn't a clue what to recommend for piles or a cold or whatever problem the person asking him had.

And all the time he was wondering who could possibly have made such a mistake on the accounts. He could understand someone skimming a few pounds here and there, but doing something that would put Bess at risk of no longer being able to run was unthinkable. It had to be a genuine mistake.

Except that a mistake would surely have shown up in the difference between the passenger numbers and the income from ticket sales. Someone must have pocketed the extra money, because it wasn't in any of the financial statements so far as he could tell.

He'd like to get Ryan's take on it, though, because Ryan seemed to understand this stuff.

And that was another mystery he'd like to clear up—Ryan drove trains for a living. How on earth did he know about all this business accounting? He was still wondering about that when Beaky told him to clean up after a kid who'd been sick in the consulting room. It happened once or twice a year, and Sam always tried to be charitable towards the person because he was pretty sure cleaning up vomit was marginally more pleasant than being the one to throw up everywhere, but sometimes he *hated* his job.

After scrubbing his hands about fifty times in the loos, even though he'd worn a pair of rubber gloves during the clean up, Sam headed out. And damn it, because of some projectile-vomiting kid, he was late and he might even miss Ryan—it was half six already and by the time he got the bus to the station, it would be nearer seven, and he didn't know where Ryan lived. He willed the bus to be on time for once.

Of course it wasn't. By the time he got off opposite the station, he was sure Ryan would be long gone, but he went in anyway to check. Sure enough, Bess's shed was locked up, there was no answer when he tapped on the staffroom door, and the only signs of life were some tired-looking people waiting for evening trains.

Disappointment bloomed deep inside him. He'd so hoped for another evening of having Ryan's company, of laughter and easy conversation. Instead of which, he'd be heading home for an evening where his only company was through the screen of his laptop. And maybe Mabel, if she turned up early.

He headed out of the station. The evening was warm and he'd just pulled off his tie to undo the top buttons of his shirt when he saw Ryan sitting at the bottom of the steps to the car park. He fought the urge to rub his eyes before looking again, because there was no way the guy would be waiting for him. But as he drew nearer, it was definitely Ryan, leaning against the wall in the evening sunshine.

"Hi," Sam said as he got closer, and despite his attempt to sound casual, excitement came through loud and clear in his voice.

Ryan stirred, opening his eyes, and it took him a moment to focus on Sam. That moment was long enough for Sam to see there was blood running from his nose.

"What the—are you okay?" he asked, urgently, crouching down in front of Ryan and looking into his face. "What happened?"

"I'm fine," Ryan said, but however defiantly he said it, he didn't move from where he was sitting.

"What happened?" Sam repeated. He rooted in his pocket, desperately hoping for a handkerchief or tissue or something, but all he could find was his tie. "Here," he said, proffering it in Ryan's direction.

Ryan's eyes narrowed on it, then he looked at Sam, and thank *God*, he started to look like Ryan again, rather than the not-quite-there stranger he'd been seconds earlier. "What, you think I need smartening up?"

"It's for the blood," Sam said.

Ryan frowned. He reached up a hand and ran it over his face, which had a nasty graze down one cheek, and ended up wiping his hand under his nose. "Huh," he said, staring down at the blood on his hand.

Sam was looking at the hole in the knee of Ryan's jeans, which was most definitely not a designer-made rip but instead an ugly jagged hole, and putting two and two together.

"Did you fall down the steps?" he asked. "Oh God, did you hit your head? Your back? You should go to hospital."

He was digging in his pocket for his phone, because he should probably call an ambulance, when Ryan spoke. "I didn't fall," he said. "I was pushed."

"What?" Sam looked up from his phone, everything else forgotten. "Who?" He looked around, but apart from a couple of people walking past on the other side of the street who weren't paying them the least bit of attention, he couldn't see anyone. "Was it on purpose?"

"Given he pushed me with his fist to my nose, I'd say it was," Ryan said wryly. He reached up and wrapped his hand around the metal handrail his head had been resting against, and pulled himself to his feet, hissing between his teeth. Once there, he looked far from stable and was blinking as he started to feel in the pockets of his jeans. "Fuck it," he said. "Get my jacket, will you?"

Ryan's leather jacket was lying halfway up the steps. Sam retrieved it.

"Bastard took my keys and wallet," Ryan said. "Check for my phone?"

At least that was there. "You were *mugged*," Sam said, horrified as it dawned on him. "In broad daylight. In *Cardale*."

"No shit, Sherlock," Ryan said, but his voice sounded resigned rather than angry.

"We have to report it to the police," Sam said.

Ryan pushed himself away from the rail he'd been holding on to. "No," he said. "No coppers. I just need to get the bank to stop my cards and—oh, fuck." He looked at Sam, sudden misery in his face. "See if my bike's still there?"

"So long as you stay here and don't go anywhere," Sam said. As Ryan closed his eyes again and just stood there looking defeated, he ran up the steps as fast as he could go. To his amazement—and relief—that huge shiny motorbike was in the parking space closest to the top of the stairs, with Ryan's helmet safely locked to it.

"It's still there," he said, coming back down, and didn't miss the way Ryan slumped with relief. "What sort of a mugger takes your keys but not your bike?"

"A crappy one," Ryan said. "Probably just wanted my wallet but took the keys because they were there. Oh hell. I need to get back to the flat, check he hasn't turned the place over."

"Where do you live?" Sam asked.

"Market Square."

Ryan looked half-dead, definitely not up to walking or catching the bus back there. "Stay here," Sam said. "I'll get my car."

The way Ryan simply sat back down on the steps again, without a word of protest, worried Sam more than anything. He sprinted up the road, wondering if he should just take Ryan to hospital once he had him in the car, because what if he'd hit his head? He might end up having one of those brain bleeds that all the patients in the medical dramas seemed to get just as they were being checked out of hospital.

Sam put on an extra burst of speed as he turned into his street.

If he hadn't got to know Ryan over the past few days, Sam would have thought nothing was wrong. As it was, Ryan was quiet and subdued and, most worryingly, did what Sam suggested. He wondered if he was hurt worse than he was letting on. Then he wondered if he was in shock. But when Sam slowed the car at the turn-off to the hospital, Ryan put his hand on the door handle and threatened to get out. So Sam took him home instead.

Ryan's place turned out to be one of the palatial Georgian houses in the town square that had been sold to a property developer a few years back and turned into flats, selling at a price few locals could afford. Ryan had roused long enough to tell Sam to Google the managing agent and a woman in a smart black suit met them at the front door and gave Ryan a new set of keys.

Once through the door, Sam formed a vague impression of high ceilings and white walls and lots of space, but he was more concerned with Ryan right then, because he was taking his jacket from Sam's hand and thanking him for the lift. As if Sam was supposed just to leave.

"I'm not going anywhere," Sam said.

"For fuck's sake." Ryan sounded exhausted. "I don't want you here."

Sam's stomach hollowed with hurt. But as he saw how ill Ryan looked, he stood his ground and tried to ignore the ache deep inside him.

"You might have a concussion," he said stubbornly. "I won't get in your way, but I'm not leaving and finding out you fell asleep on your couch and died because no one noticed you lapsing into a coma."

Ryan sank down on the brown leather couch as if his legs wouldn't hold him any longer. "Whatever."

Sam stood looking at him and wondered just how much pain he was in. "Do you want an aspirin? Or a cup of tea? Or something to eat?"

"Some water," Ryan said. He leaned against the squashy back of the couch and closed his eyes.

RYAN

Sam had finally stopped hovering. Ryan reckoned he'd have a few minutes peace and quiet before he was back, because he'd have to find his way around the kitchen cupboards, looking for a glass. That suited him down to the ground.

He felt stupid as hell for not seeing the mugging coming, and even more embarrassed that he'd been so out of it that he didn't remember the guy nicking his wallet and keys. God, he'd been a sitting duck. He deserved to be hurt worse than he was, with just a headache that threatened to explode behind his eyes and a body that felt sore all over. At least his bike was safe, he realized belatedly, as the guy wouldn't know which vehicle the keys were for.

Sam was back almost before he had time to breathe, and he was doing that hovering thing again. For God's sake. All Ryan wanted was to be left in peace to lick his wounds. So he sent Sam off into the spare bedroom to look through the crates he still hadn't unpacked till he found the one with paperwork in it, because he'd need to get the bank to stop his cards.

He didn't care about Sam poking through his stuff. He hadn't got anything personal, not really, and his sex toys had been among the first things to be unpacked and were now in a neat case under his bed. It was a bit of a shame—he'd give anything to witness Sam finding them and slowly working out what they were. He was willing to bet that confusion would be followed by embarrassment, followed by those dark eyes of his suddenly brightening as he thought about using them with Ryan.

He was still smiling when he drifted off to sleep.

"You can't go into work today."

Sam was doing that stubborn thing with his chin as he stood at the foot of the bed. His hands were on his hips and his whole stance screamed determination, which looked less than impressive as he was naked except for a pair of faded red-and-white-spotted boxers. He'd kept them on last night in some sort of burst of modesty. It was probably because they hadn't had sex. He'd ended up staying because Ryan had sighed and said it was obvious he wasn't going anywhere so he might as well stay and make sure Ryan didn't expire in his sleep.

As Ryan sank back down on the bed with a groan, he had to concede Sam might have a point. He felt like he'd been trampled by a herd of elephants. The thought of even *getting* to work, let alone the physical work of driving Bessie and concentrating through the headache he still had, made rolling back under the covers very inviting right now. But...

"If I call in sick, I'm just giving Cleaver another excuse. Not to mention it'll take them a couple of hours to get Roger here to replace me, so Bessie will be late today."

"He can't fire you over being sick," Sam said. "Especially not when you're covered in bruises so *no one* could think you're faking it." His gaze flicked over Ryan's less than attractive body, with blotchy patches of green and yellow beginning to show. His lips thinned in disapproval, but his eyes were soft and worried on Ryan's face.

Something tugged deep inside Ryan, the way it had last night when he'd woken up in the living room to find he'd somehow ended up collapsed on the sofa with his head in Sam's lap. Sam was just sitting there in the dark, his hand moving slowly and comfortingly over Ryan's shoulder. It had been so unlike anything Ryan had known that he'd of course had to get up and make a joke of things, but later, in bed, with the light out and rain soft against the window, he'd moved close against Sam and somehow they'd ended up holding one another. Ryan figured his head injury was enough excuse, though even that didn't explain the way he breathed Sam's name at one point. He'd tensed after it was out, hoping to God Sam was actually asleep and hadn't heard. Sam said nothing, and did nothing, so Ryan thought he'd got away with it. Which was fine, right up until he was drifting off to sleep and Sam placed the softest of kisses against his temple.

But that gentle, quiet Sam was a world away right now. He was a man on a mission, and all of a sudden Ryan had a flash of what he must look like hunting down missing engines to complete his collection of numbers or whatever it was trainspotters did. Maybe he was getting confused with Monopoly. Head injury. He was allowed.

Somehow it was easier to give in to Sam and allow himself to be organised, with his phone carefully placed on the bedside table next to a mug of tea. Sam had checked the battery was charged so that Ryan could call him at any time in the day if he felt like he might be about to die or just needed a refill on the tea. Ryan used it to call Simon and let him know he wouldn't be in, and by the time Sam came back from the bathroom, he had rolled himself under the covers again. Sam had one eye anxiously on his watch because free parking in the square ran out at 7 a.m. and the traffic wardens in Cardale were *ferocious*, but he still lingered by the side of the bed, looking reluctant to leave, until Ryan told him to get lost.

When the door closed behind Sam, he reached out for his phone to see if he had any messages. Anything to distract himself from the way the flat felt suddenly quiet and too big without Sam there.

SAM

Sam was ten minutes late for work, which meant a lecture from Beaky and the prospect of making up the time during his lunch break. But he couldn't regret it too much, because he'd had to make sure Ryan was okay before leaving him. He was pretty sure that Ryan was out of danger now, having looked up online the symptoms of concussion and other delayed effects from falls, but it hadn't felt right to leave him on his own when his one and only attempt to get out of bed had left him hobbling around like a geriatric tortoise.

He checked his phone during his coffee break, but there was no text from Ryan. He didn't know if that was good or bad. Either he was asleep or he'd died in his sleep. And even Sam had to snort at his logic. No, the much more likely answer was that Ryan hadn't given him another thought once he'd left. Even so, he sent a text just asking if Ryan was okay.

He got a response almost immediately. *Stop fussing.*

And before he knew how he should take that, another one pinged through. *You want to pick up Indian tonight?*

Sam didn't stop grinning for the rest of the day.

Chapter Ten

RYAN

By the time Sam finally arrived that evening, Ryan was *starving*. He'd slept most of the day away, though he had managed to have a hot shower, which seemed to have eased some of his stiffness, and he'd also got a locksmith in to change the locks on his door just in case the bastard who'd nicked his keys managed to track down where he lived. In the middle of all that, he'd somehow forgotten to eat.

Sam made himself a cup of tea while Ryan dug into the plastic bag he'd brought with him that was filled with cartons of Indian food, the rich, spicy smell taunting him even before he got the first lid off. The carton was filled with little rough balls of onion bhajis and, unable to wait a second longer, he picked one out and stuffed it in his mouth. And practically came on the spot.

"Bloody hell," he said. "That's amazing." He picked up another one and bit it in half, to find it was equally as good. "Try it," he said, closing the few steps between them and pushing it between

Sam's lips. Sam, taken by surprise, opened so readily and easily for him that it took Ryan's mind off food and somewhere else entirely.

"Good," Sam agreed, once he'd chewed and swallowed. "Vihaan makes them specially—"

But Ryan couldn't give a flying fuck what Vihaan did or didn't do. He was pressing Sam back against the counter with his body and kissing him. And God, Sam felt good. His lips were soft and tentative, but it didn't take long for Ryan to turn the kiss into something more, something wet and deep and filthy, until Sam was rutting against him, making demanding noises in his throat.

Ryan pulled down the zipper of the black trousers Sam wore for work and worked his way inside, until that hot hard length was in his hand and Sam made a high-pitched gasp before launching his own assault on Ryan's jeans. They were jacking one another off, no finesse and precious little technique, just need and urgency as they kissed.

And when Sam went off, the sound he made into Ryan's mouth had Ryan wrapping his hand around Sam's and frantically working himself until God, that was it, he was done.

He came to a few moments later, head resting against Sam's shoulder, breathing at last returned to normal, and choked a laugh as he saw what a mess they'd made.

"Fuck," he said, groping for the kitchen roll on the top behind Sam. He mopped at the spunk on Sam's black trousers but gave up when that didn't seem to do much good and concentrated on making himself decent. "Dinner better not have got cold," he said, as he ran his hand under the tap. Sam jostled him to one side, and Ryan, surprised for an instant at Sam's pushiness, suddenly remembered—no one came between Sam and his food.

"It's your own fault if it is," Sam said virtuously, but his attempt to sound self-righteous was undermined by the grin on his face. "I'll have to get onion bhajis again if you like them that much."

"Seriously, they're never usually that good."

Sam looked up from where he'd started taking the lids off cartons. "Don't tell me you go to the Star of India."

Ryan laid two plates out on the top. "If that's the one on the marketplace."

"Oh hell, don't do that, not if you want to live. I reckon the only reason it's still going is because all the drunks eat there when the pubs kick out. You need the Rosebud, up that street behind the DIY shop. It looks like a dump, but it has the *best* food. I forgot you're new here—you need someone to show you around."

The problem was, if Ryan got sacked, he wouldn't be staying here. He didn't know where he'd go. Ryan picked up his full plate, but suddenly his appetite was gone.

The feeling of melancholy had disappeared by the time they'd finished the best Indian meal Ryan had had since leaving London and Sam had told him of the discrepancy he'd uncovered in the accounts. Ryan in turn told of his own discovery about the non-existent supplier, which had left Sam wide-eyed with shock.

"But who would *do* that?" he demanded. "Who on earth would risk it? All it would take would be one question and the whole thing would come tumbling down."

Ryan felt about fifty years older than Sam in that moment. "People don't tend to ask questions, because they think like you do—they trust people are what they seem," he said. The meal lay uneasily in his stomach as he realised that was precisely what Sam was doing with *him*. Sam just had to ask the right question, and Ryan's whole sordid past would come out.

"So what do we do now?" Sam asked. "I mean, should we go to the police? Or there must be some sort of charities body we could report this to."

Bleakness swamped Ryan. "There's nothing we can do. Who the hell's going to listen to a disgruntled soon-to-be-ex-employee?"

"We could tell the trustee board," Sam said, eyes alight with challenge.

"Who are they going to listen to? The guy they appointed—the guy whose accounts they've signed off on for the past three years, putting their reputations, not to mention legal liability, on the line—or the new guy, who by the way is about to be fired and couldn't possibly be trying to make trouble in retaliation?"

"You're wrong," Sam insisted. "There must be something we can do. Someone we can tell. Go to the police. They'd have a duty to investigate if we can show them where the accounts don't add up."

Ryan snorted as he levered himself to his feet, bruises protesting at the movement. "As if your average copper's going to understand management accounts," he said, heading into the kitchen. "You want a beer?"

"Okay," Sam said, sounding uncertain. And when Ryan came back out with a couple of cans, he was frowning down at the account printouts he'd picked up from the pile on the floor, his brow knotted. "There has to be *something* we can do," he said again when Ryan pressed the beer into his hand.

"Well, there isn't," Ryan said, and felt bad about the way Sam shrank into himself at his tone. He sat back down, hissing as his bruises yet again made themselves known.

"I spoke to my boss today," Sam said, and the complete change of subject had Ryan mentally scrambling to keep up. "I asked him what's best for bruises and stiffness following a fall, and he said—"

"Why the hell would your boss know that?"

"I work in the pharmacy department," Sam said. "And he said that even though usually only old ladies buy them now, Epsom salts are the best thing there is to ease stiffness because as well as reducing swelling, they do something to the nervous system, sedate it or something. So, I, uh, got some for you if you want to try them in the bath."

The words tumbled quickly from Sam's mouth, as if he was unsure if he was overstepping by saying them, and it took Ryan a moment to untangle his meaning. And then he wasn't sure whether to laugh or bang his head against the closest surface. Because Sam really *was* an old woman in a hot young guy's body. But at the same time, something inside Ryan warmed at the fact that he'd thought about Ryan and gone to this trouble.

"I'll try them," he said.

Which he thought was enough, except Sam was up and going to the bag he'd left in the hallway on arrival before appearing in the doorway, expectantly holding a jar of white crystals. As if he was expecting Ryan to have a bath here and now.

Ryan didn't understand how it happened, but there was something in Sam's puppy-like expectation that led him to lever himself painfully up once more and head to the bathroom, where he started stripping off—slowly, because raising his arms above his head to get his T-shirt off hurt like hell—and Sam ran a bath, tipping out some of those crystals into the running water. Maybe Sam was some sort of serial killer who murdered his victims in an acid bath and the innocent act was simply a cover.

Sam swirled his hand around to disperse the crystals, which at least put paid to the acid possibility, then straightened up and looked round. "Bloody *hell*," he said as he saw Ryan's naked body. It wasn't the admiring way most guys said it—he sounded appalled. "Is there an inch of you that isn't bruised?"

"I dunno," Ryan drawled, his hand skimming his belly and lower, till his fingers rested on his cock. "These nine inches seem okay to me. Maybe you'd like to check. With your mouth."

Sam's eyes brightened with laughter at Ryan's offer—which actually, had started as a joke but was beginning to sound really good. But sadly, even that wasn't enough to put Sam off his aim of getting Ryan into that bath.

Ryan wanted to object to being treated like a five-year-old, but the way the warm water felt as he gingerly leaned back in the bath was too damn good for him to bear any resentment. God, it felt amazing.

It felt even better when, after fifteen minutes soaking, somehow Sam ended up on his knees next to the bathtub, kissing Ryan hot and messily while he stroked him off in the water. After that, Ryan felt too relaxed to move. He tried to reciprocate, because he could see Sam was hard in his trousers, but Sam simply shook his head and helped him get out of the bath—and no, Ryan wasn't fucking helpless, but the mix of Epsom salts and a good orgasm had him so droopy he could hardly stand upright.

He drew the line at Sam actually drying him. Instead he swiped the towel in the approximate direction of his body and staggered off in search of his bed. He couldn't remember when he'd last slept this much. He hoped it was his body catching up on sleep, rather than the result of some lurking head injury from his fall.

He was vaguely aware of Sam letting down the blinds, then getting undressed himself, ready to join him under the sheet. He thought he'd do something about that hard-on of Sam's once he got into bed. Life was a series of transactions—no one did anything without expecting payback. He was still waiting for Sam to join him so he could discharge his debt when he fell asleep.

SAM

The next morning, Sam left Ryan in bed. Apparently it was his day off, when the relief driver Roger came in from Port Heath to drive Bess. Sam was glad about that because he didn't think Ryan would have taken another day off otherwise and he needed more time to recover. He was also disappointed, because he'd agreed to shift his own days off to Thursday and Friday this week to let Denise have time off for half-term. If he hadn't done that, he could have spent the whole day with Ryan.

He was still thinking about Ryan when he was up in the stock room, doing the stock-take that he always got volunteered for because everyone hated doing it. Sam didn't understand why Ryan wouldn't go to the police. He considered taking their discoveries to them no matter what Ryan thought about it. But Ryan's attitude had had an effect on him; he thought someone could easily explain the carriage error as a genuine mix-up, and as for the fake company that Ryan was so certain existed, they had no proof.

He sighed as he finished the stock-take at long last and signed the last form. They had to do *something*, or Ryan would lose his job. Then he'd leave Cardale. And Bess would stop running.

"Melanie wants you to cover the tills during coffee break." Dawn's voice jerked him back to the present. She was standing by the lift, a pack of cigarettes in her hand, obviously on her way for her own break.

"Okay," Sam said obediently. And then it struck him, an idea so blinding in its brilliance he almost gasped. "Dawn? Can I talk to you for a minute?"

RYAN

Ryan was bored. He usually took the bike out on his day off if the weather was good, but having recovered it from the staff car park with his spare key, he found that riding it pulled at the bruising over his ribs. Taking it out on the swooping bends and hills around Cardale would be more of a stamina test than fun. And there was no point looking at those damn accounts any more, not now he knew there was nothing he could do about them. Which left him at a bit of a loose end.

That was why early afternoon saw him walking into Braddons, looking for the pharmacy department. Not because he particularly wanted to see Sam, but because he couldn't think of anything else to do. When he eventually found the right section—the shop turned out to be a rabbit warren filled with unexpected staircases and hidden corners—there was no sign of Sam.

Well, it wasn't as if he was in any hurry. He wandered through into the next section, to find it was stuffed with postcards and boxes of fudge declaring *With love from Cardale*. He couldn't quite believe what he was seeing. No one would choose to come here, surely. There was nothing in this town except for Bessie.

That was when he saw the watercolour of her hanging in pride of place on the wall, her livery gleaming maroon and gold as she puffed her way through rolling hills. It was allegedly by a "renowned local artist", though Ryan didn't think it would pass muster as anything more than a pretty little daub anywhere other than Cardale. But something about the way the artist had caught the light on her meant he kept looking at it, until he gave in and bought it, though he knew he'd only end up throwing it away because he didn't do sentimentality. The guy at the till wrapped it in acres of bubble wrap as if it was something precious, not a crappy picture that only cost a few hundred quid.

With it tucked awkwardly under his arm, he went back into the pharmacy and immediately spotted Sam's dark head, about a foot above everyone else's, even though it was bent as he listened attentively to whatever the woman talking to him was saying. Something he'd rather not know about, Ryan thought, drifting close enough to catch the words "flaking skin" and "rashes".

How did Sam do it, working here? And *why*? There probably weren't that many job opportunities in a town like this, but at the same time, he could have worked in a clothes store or something, not this place that looked like it had outstayed its welcome by a couple of decades.

Moving away again while he waited for Sam to be free, he saw a notice pointing up the stairs. *Gentlemen's Clothing*, it said, and he shuddered, wondering what the hell sort of clothes this place sold. And then it clicked into place. This was undoubtedly where Sam got those godawful jeans from. Shit. He'd have to do something about them, that was for sure. It was a crime to have an arse like Sam's and not show it off.

"Can I help you?"

The voice came from a blonde woman in her mid-forties. He realised he'd been standing stock still as he thought about what Sam looked like with no clothes to spoil the view.

"Just browsing, thanks," he said, then saw he was in front of the contraceptives counter.

"Er, actually," he said, as she turned to walk away. "I'm—er, is there a male member of staff I could talk to about this?"

Her eyes softened when she saw his innocent embarrassment—a look he'd stolen directly from Sam. "Of course," she said. "Just a minute."

She sent Sam in his direction, stepping in to deal with the old bat with the flaking skin herself. Ryan positioned himself behind the head-high display, so it wasn't until Sam rounded the corner of the counter that he saw Ryan. His mouth dropped open.

"Maybe you can help me," Ryan said, waving a couple of packets of condoms under Sam's nose. "I mean, there's ribbed, and dotted, and the ones with the tingly fresh feeling of mint, and frankly there's so many I really don't know which to try first. What would you recommend?"

Sam's face was rigid as he stared over at the pharmacy counter. "Beaky has a fit if we talk to friends at work," he hissed.

"But I'm a customer." Ryan sent Sam one of his best glinting smiles. "A customer who needs help. I mean, how do *you* feel about ribbed versus dotted?"

Sam spluttered. "I—I don't know," he said. He pulled himself together with an effort as the woman Ryan had spoken to walked past the end of the counter, her eyes cutting over to look at them for an instant. "Everyone has different tastes."

Ryan leaned in closer, hoping it looked as if he didn't want to be overheard because he was embarrassed. "But for the sake of argument, let's say it was *you* I was going to fuck tonight. What if I were to spread you out on my bed and fuck you with my fingers until you're begging for my cock. Which would you want more—the feeling of each ribbed band as my big cock pushes slowly inside you, the anticipation as you wait for the next one and the rippling feel as I move in and out, or something that's less predictable, so when I start to really fuck you, you never know just when one of the dots is going to hit you just where it matters?"

Sam's mouth was opening and closing like a fish out of water, his colour high, but most interesting of all was the way the front of his trousers were suddenly all out of shape.

"I mean, that's before we even start on all the different lubes," Ryan said. "There's the warming one, which starts off low, but God, when it gets going it's amazing, or there's different flavours which I could lick—"

"I think you should get everything," Sam said, pulling handfuls of stuff at random from the display and pressing them into Ryan's hands. Ryan couldn't tell if the tightness in his voice was from embarrassment or arousal.

"XXL?" he asked, looking at the box on top of the huge pile he was now holding. "I'd say I'm flattered, but actually, it's true."

"If that's everything, sir," Sam said, and the *sir* slammed through Ryan's gut like nothing he'd ever known. He'd never been interested in that side of things before, just liking a good, simple suck or fuck, but the thought of role-playing with Sam, who he knew he could trust absolutely...

"I'll let you know how my experiments go," he said with a smirk.

As he paid for the mountain of sex aids Sam had pressed on him, he heard a clatter. Glancing back, he found Sam had managed to knock a whole shelf of stuff off the display and was crouching down to pick all the boxes up.

Ryan's smirk turned into a full-blown grin. He couldn't tell if Sam had done it to give his erection time to subside before he had to venture out from behind the shelter of the counter or if Ryan had got him so worked up that he'd lost coordination. Either way, he was extremely pleased with his afternoon's work.

SAM

Sam spent the rest of the afternoon in a state of low-grade arousal, and by the time he was finally hammering on Ryan's front door, it had turned into something much more hungry and immediate. The instant Ryan opened the door, Sam was pushing him back against the wall, hands working at the belt on Ryan's jeans as he kissed him, intent on wiping that smirk off his face.

Sam had no idea how things went from him trying to get into Ryan's jeans to finding himself naked on his back on Ryan's rather large bed. Ryan was over him, holding him still as his mouth mapped a line over his chest and his stomach, before sliding down on his cock, wet and welcoming and like heaven.

Sam's hands were in Ryan's hair, and he was trying so hard not to push Ryan's head down or to buck up into his mouth. Ryan seemed to know how damn difficult he was finding it because he put one hand on Sam's hip to hold him steady as he set up a rhythm that was just too slow to be perfect, because Sam wanted *more*. And Ryan seemed to know that too, because his fingers were sliding deep inside him, opening him up. Sam whimpered at the promise of what he'd been imagining all afternoon. But his imagination had nothing on reality, with Ryan's hard cock filling him until he could scarcely breathe at how good it felt so deep inside him.

"*Please,*" he got out between broken breaths, and Ryan finally gave him exactly what he wanted—thrusting deep and fast, one hand closing around Sam's cock until he came, helpless and shuddering.

It only took a few more thrusts, grown wild and unrhythmic, before Ryan was swearing and shooting his load. He collapsed on top of Sam, who couldn't do anything but hold him and try to breathe.

"Fuck," Ryan said at last. Extricating himself, he removed the condom and flung it at the bin before lying back down beside Sam, seeming almost as floppy as Sam felt right now. The bed was bathed in sunshine through the big sash window, lighting Ryan's skin where it gleamed with sweat, and bruises or no bruises, Sam didn't think he'd ever seen anything so beautiful.

He traced a line along Ryan's muscled arm and thought about him driving Bess, about the way he'd held Sam down just now, strong but careful, and he knew he was in love.

Chapter Eleven

RYAN

Ryan was back at work the next day. Every time Marlene saw him, she checked anxiously that he was well enough to be there. He'd been thankful to find that the blow to his nose hadn't resulted in a black eye, and the superficial graze on his cheek was almost gone, meaning he didn't have to confess the humiliation of being mugged in broad daylight. Instead he let them all assume it was some twenty-four-hour bug he'd had.

Marlene gave him some mints with a picture of Bess on the packaging "in case he had a sore throat". If she was that open-handed with everyone, he couldn't understand how the gift shop made any money. He took them with a word of thanks, only for Simon to grin broadly when he saw them later.

"You're going to have to put her out of her misery," he said.

Ryan stared at him. He was usually hyper-aware of the effect he had on people, but Marlene must have been sixty if she was a day.

A very well-preserved sixty, who enjoyed wearing tight dresses and a *lot* of jewellery, but still. He'd missed it. He must be slipping.

It was a busy day. The schools' half-term holiday meant the platform was heaving by the afternoon, filled with excited schoolkids and harassed parents, and Ryan was more thankful than he could say that he was safely on Bessie's footplate, where the general public were strictly forbidden to venture.

Eventually, after so many turns around the loop he was starting to feel dizzy, they'd finished the trips for the day. When the last passengers were finally clear of the carriages and making their noisy way across the footbridge, he looked for Amit's signal that he was clear to take Bessie back to her shed, and saw an anxious-looking guy standing on the platform, a small boy holding his hand as they both stared at him. The guy waved at Ryan when he saw him. Usually Ryan would have just waved back, but the anxiety in this guy's body language had him glancing to Simon to let him know he was in charge for now, and climbing down to go and see what the guy wanted.

The expression on the little boy's face as he approached was never going to get old. Some days the awe in which the kids held him made Ryan feel like a figure from legend.

"Josh wanted to say thank you for today's ride," the man said. "Oh, sorry, I should introduce myself—I'm Gerald Heath and this is Joshua, and he's been saving his pocket money for the past month so we could come today."

Well, that explained the guy's anxiety—he wanted to make sure the kid had the best day possible and hadn't been sure if Ryan would talk to them. The little boy was clutching at his dad's hand and seemed too overpowered to speak.

Ryan crouched down in front of him. "Is that right?" he asked. "You like trains, Josh?"

"They're the best," he burst out. "And Bess is *beautiful*. I'm going to be an engine driver when I grow up."

"You do that," Ryan said. He saw Marlene locking the gift shop and realised that by hanging around in the hope of talking to him, Josh would have lost the opportunity to get a piece of cheap tat to remind him of today's treat. "Tell you what," he said, "why don't I give you a head start?"

He pulled the engine driver cap off his head and placed it on Josh's. It was far too big for him, tipping so that the peak of the cap obscured one of his eyes, but the way the visible eye was shining meant he obviously didn't care.

"I better put Bessie to bed," he said, standing up. "You take care, Josh."

The hat jiggled dangerously with the force of Josh's nod.

"Thank you so much," the dad, whose name Ryan had already forgotten, said quietly. He put out a hand, which Ryan found a little odd, but he shook it to be polite. "I don't care what they say about you—that was a really nice thing you just did."

He turned and shepherded Josh away, a job made more difficult by the fact that Josh kept turning every few steps to look back and wave madly at Ryan and then have to push his hat back up so he could see again. Ryan was too busy trying to work out what the hell the dad had been talking about to wave back at first.

When Josh, who was now excitedly chattering away to his dad, turned one last time at the foot of the bridge, Ryan managed to wave back at him before climbing onto Bessie. What they said about him? It wasn't like anyone here knew who he was. Saunders was a pretty common name, and Ryan Saunders equally so. No one would have a reason to connect him with *that* Ryan Saunders. So what the hell had the guy meant? He guessed he must have overheard some of the staff bitching about him being gay, because he didn't hide it and he knew some of them probably said shit about it behind his back. He shook off his disquiet, blew the whistle as a warning they were about to move and eased the throttle open to take Bessie back to her home.

SAM

The afternoon dragged by so slowly that Sam wondered at one point if his watch had actually stopped. It wasn't as if Ryan had said anything about meeting up tonight, but Sam couldn't imagine they *wouldn't*. He could just pop into the station on the way home and pretend he was indulging his passion for trainspotting. A passion which seemed to have fallen by the wayside for the past week or so.

He still loved trains, and he knew he always would. It was just that he no longer needed them to fill his life. He had something else now. He didn't think Ryan was interested in a relationship, but it seemed to Sam that they had fallen into one anyway. And if he didn't draw Ryan's attention to that fact, maybe by the time Ryan realised, he might not want it to end.

He was probably living in a fool's paradise—one of Uncle Ken's sayings—but since the alternative was spending every minute wondering when it would end, he decided to continue living there. Because Ryan was wonderful. He was everything Sam had ever dreamed of, and so much more.

The instant Beaky finally locked the doors, Sam headed out to the bus stop. He really had to get the grin off his face before he got to the station—even *he* didn't usually get this excited about the evening commuter trains and it would be a dead giveaway to Ryan that Sam wasn't really there for them.

He was practically hopping with impatience waiting for the bus when he noticed the guy next to him had a copy of the *Cardale Evening Chronicle* under his arm. He couldn't *believe* he'd forgotten—he blamed Ryan, actually, for distracting him so thoroughly yesterday afternoon. Ryan's visit to the contraceptive counter had driven everything else out of his head, including his chat with Dawn and the way she'd called her dad at the *Chronicle's* offices so Sam could talk to him about Bess.

Glancing swiftly up the road to check there was no sign of his bus, he dived into the nearby newsagents, snatched up a copy, paid and was back, all without losing his place in the queue. He knew they might not have published anything this soon, but he also knew what a huge fan of Bess Dawn's father was and reckoned that, barring murder and mayhem on the town's streets, he'd have prioritised this story. Sam hadn't dared mention anything about the accounts to him, because that way lay slander charges, but had said he'd been told that Bess's driver was in danger of losing his job due to financial difficulties with the trust. And whatever else happened, just printing that publicly would surely have the trustees looking into their finances properly, if only to refute the paper's charge.

Even though he knew it was too soon realistically to expect anything, he was still disappointed to scan the front page and see nothing. Until he saw the box with the highlights of the paper's contents and the tagline: *Old Bess—does she deserve better? See page 3*. He opened the paper, stomach knotted with excitement, only to stare in disbelief at what he saw. Yes, there was a big spread on page three, but it was...oh *God*. What had he *done*?

Sam reeled away from the queue, desperate to get away from other people. Safely round the corner, hiding in the doorway of a closed charity shop, he read it properly. But however many times he read it—and he did, over and over again—it didn't make any more sense than it had the first time.

The words still jumped out at him, words about Ryan. Tales of drunkenness and drugs, of wild behaviour at exclusive nightclubs and sex tapes online paled alongside the other things—a *prison sentence*, and assault charges that were only dropped because of his father's influence. (Allegedly. The *Chronicle* was covering its arse.)

Even *Sam* had heard of John Saunders, the entrepreneur who was practically the poster-boy for what the Government called "Go-ahead Britain". The John Saunders who, according to the *Chronicle*, had finally washed his hands of his good-for-nothing son a year ago. Ryan hadn't been seen at any of his usual high-profile haunts since. His sudden disappearance from the gossip columns of the tabloids had caused a few eyebrows to be raised.

The answer to what had happened to Ryan Saunders was quite simple, the article went on to explain—he was here in Cardale, responsible for the town's most treasured possession. The paper didn't come out and *say* it, but it didn't have to because the implication was obvious. He couldn't be trusted with Bess.

Sam kept swallowing, but the bile in his throat wouldn't go away. It couldn't be true. Except there was a picture of a younger Ryan, obviously out of his gourd, flashing an obscene gesture at the photographer. That was with one hand; the other was snaking into the waistband of the good-looking guy he was with, his intentions only too obvious.

Sam sank into a trembling crouch. He didn't know how it had happened, but somehow Dawn's father had twisted everything. Sam had only wanted the paper to report on Bess being under financial threat. He hadn't thought there was anything wrong with answering questions about a few facts, like the name of the driver who'd been told about the financial situation, just so long as he didn't say anything about Mr Cleaver or the accounts. But somehow, instead of saving Ryan's job, Sam had pretty well *ensured* he'd lost it.

Oh God. *Ryan*. He had to find some way to tell Ryan what he'd done. A Ryan who he didn't think he knew any more, not after what he'd read.

RYAN

Ryan had almost finished with Bessie and Simon had already left when Cleaver showed up. The instant Ryan saw him, every instinct kicked into overdrive because he looked like a cat who'd got the cream, the canary, and evicted the dog all at once.

"Thought you could hang me out to dry in the court of public opinion, did you?" Cleaver asked.

Ryan said nothing because firstly, he hadn't a bloody *clue* what the old git was on about, and secondly, he knew from years of dealing with his father the one thing a guy like that hated more than anything was not getting a reaction. He carried on rubbing the cloth over Bessie's side, restoring her to a perfect shine.

"The thing is, Saunders, I have more powerful friends than you. And I don't have a past to be splashed all over the papers. You think the trustees are going to want to keep you now? I'm expecting an outraged phone call any second asking if I knew about your criminal record when I hired you."

Ryan didn't know what the hell was going on, but it definitely wasn't good. "It was on my application."

"Oh, sure." Cleaver's smile showed a lot of teeth. "I'm a great believer in rehabilitation and second chances. But when it's added to your erratic attendance these past few days, turning up late and then not at all, I'm going to have to regretfully agree with the trustees that, while I did a good thing in offering you a second chance, you're not the right person for the job."

Helpless fury was a tight ball in Ryan's gut. Pressure from the trustees meant Cleaver could fire him without any questions being asked, whereas if Cleaver had just sacked him, months after hiring him, there might have been one or two questions about his competence in recruitment. It *might* have made Cleaver think twice about doing it, but even that faint hope was gone now.

"Whatever," he said, and rubbed harder at a piece of dirt that didn't seem to want to leave Bessie. He knew the feeling.

Cleaver snorted, turned on his heel and left. He left the door open, of course—closing doors was for the menial labour to do—and Ryan straightened up and stared after his portly figure as it disappeared up the platform. What the fuck had he been talking about, Ryan hanging him out in the court of public opinion? The only person he'd talked to about Cleaver had been Sam, and even he didn't know the full story. Ryan and Simon shared an eye-roll on occasion, but they hadn't discussed Cleaver in actual words. Mainly because they only said about ten words a day to one another, and those were usually "coal", "speed" and "pressure". Make that three words a day.

It wasn't as if Sam would have told anyone. The only friends he seemed to have were half the old-age pensioners of this town and a giant spider.

Ryan shoved the cloth in his pocket and left Bessie, even though she wasn't quite finished. He didn't have the heart to spend his time buffing her till she gleamed like he usually did. Not now losing her was imminent. He locked the shed behind him with the key Amit had given him that morning—his shed key had been part of the bunch that had been stolen—and headed up the empty platform. All he could think was that it was probably for the last time.

SAM

Sam paused at the top of the flight of stairs down to the platform, watching Ryan making his way from Bessie's shed. He looked so familiar that Sam's throat ached, because he knew now that it was all an illusion—he didn't know Ryan Saunders at all. He never had. He'd built up some sort of fantasy of his perfect guy and slotted Ryan into it.

As Sam drew a deep, unsteady breath, he realised that wasn't quite true. Nothing he'd read about Ryan in the newspaper reflected the guy he had known—someone who was cocky, but *kind*. Kinder than anyone had ever been to Sam, except for Uncle Ken and his Garden Club friends. Even Ryan's teasing about Sam's nerdiness hadn't had an edge to it, and after five years of being the class nerd at school, Sam was well aware what that sort of teasing felt like. That wasn't teasing at all—it was bullying, dressed up in apparent humour to excuse it. But Ryan wasn't like that.

The butterflies in his stomach began slowly to settle, until another thought raked them all back up again. Ryan had gone to *prison*. Sam had never known anyone who'd even been in trouble with the police, but Ryan had obviously done something really bad.

Tempting though it was to carry on standing here, his brain chasing in circles, Sam couldn't put it off any longer. He took another deep breath, squared his shoulders and started down the steps.

Ryan glanced over and saw him as he neared the bottom of the stairs. Sam knew it was cowardly, but he slowed his pace. He didn't know how to say it. He hadn't a clue how Ryan would react, but nobody was going to like having awful things about them splashed all over the local newspaper.

"What's up?" Ryan asked as they got close enough to speak without shouting down the platform at one another.

Sam guessed he looked as miserable and uncertain as he felt right now. "I've done something really stupid. But I didn't know, Ryan—I didn't know he'd ignore my story and concentrate on you instead. I swear I didn't mean it to happen."

Ryan was standing very still, his muscles coiled and tense. Despite himself, Sam remembered what that article had said about an assault charge. He held out the newspaper in a hand that wasn't quite steady.

"You'd better see for yourself," he said.

After an instant's hesitation, as if he didn't actually want to know, Ryan snatched it from Sam. His fingers clenched so hard on the paper as he read that Sam swallowed nervously, thinking of that prison sentence, but then he remembered the same hands being so careful with him, and he didn't know what to think any more. Except when Ryan raised his gaze to look at Sam, he realised whatever he thought didn't matter—he wasn't going to get a say in what happened next. The fury in Ryan's face had Sam taking a step backwards.

"You talked to a fucking reporter about me?"

"I told him you'd been warned your job was under threat because of financial pressures." It spilled out of Sam, panic-stricken. "And he asked who had told you, but I didn't like to say it was Mr Cleaver in case that was slanderous or something, but when he asked for your name, I didn't think it mattered giving him that. I didn't *know*." It ended up coming out almost like a wail, apology and upset and panic combining until Sam sounded five years old and caught with his football next to a broken window.

"I'm sorry, Ryan," he said. "So sorry."

"Well, that makes everything all right then, doesn't it?"

Sam flinched at the scathing mockery in Ryan's voice. He shook his head miserably, not knowing what else he could possibly say.

"How could you be so fucking *stupid*?" It was furious and raw and hit Sam like a freight train. "You don't *ever* talk to the press, rule number fucking one. God. You're a fucking *moron*." He cast the paper aside and stood there, breathing fast as he glared at Sam.

"I'm sorry," Sam choked out again.

Ryan shook his head. "Forget it," he said, and something in him had changed. The anger was still there, but it was overridden by weary resignation. "Just forget it. It's time I moved on from this shithole anyway."

His eyes raked over Sam in disgust, and he shook his head again before he turned and walked away.

Chapter Twelve

RYAN

Ryan opened the throttle of his bike, but the long, beckoning sweep of the bends didn't have their usual soothing effect. At last he pulled into a lay-by at the top of a hill and got off his bike. Taking his helmet off, he stood there, the slight breeze stronger up here and tugging at his hair.

Fuck it. Fuck it to hell.

Ryan had seen all the reactions there were to finding out just who he was—greed, disgust and prurience. His response was always to stick two fingers up and carry on doing whatever he wanted. But he didn't feel that way any more, not here. Things here had been different.

Not any longer, though. That fucking article in that fucking rag made it clear he would be out of a job the instant the trustees read it. Hell, *he'd* fire him.

What the hell had Sam been *thinking*? But even as he tried to whip up his anger against Sam again, he knew exactly what Sam had been thinking. He'd been trying to save Ryan's job. And, not entirely coincidentally, Bessie as well. He was like a pet goldfish swimming among sharks and not realising that was what he was doing. Of course a sleazebag like Cleaver would have contacts with all the people who mattered in this fucking town. He probably played golf every Friday afternoon with the editor of that rag.

Sam was so fucking clueless that he would never have considered the possibility the reporter might not run with the story he wanted. He trusted people. He'd trusted *Ryan,* for God's sake. If that didn't deserve a prize for cluelessness, he didn't know what did.

But shit, the road to hell was lousy with good intentions and Sam had just shoved Ryan down that road again.

He kicked the exhaust pipe on his bike. For the first time he could remember, he'd found something he wanted to do. It turned out he was good at it too. Slowly he'd started to build something around himself, something which fucking Sam Chancellor had taken a sledgehammer to and smashed to pieces.

It didn't matter what Sam's intentions had been. All that mattered was that, once again, Ryan was left with nothing.

SAM

Sam huddled in Uncle Ken's armchair and tried to breathe through the gulping, ugly sobs that shook him. His whole world was tears and snot and the pain in his chest.

He hadn't cried like this since Uncle Ken had died and he'd thought that nothing could ever hurt as much as that, but he'd been wrong. He'd lost something so precious, and it was all his fault. He might tell himself he wasn't to blame for what the paper had done with his story, but what *was* his fault, what was unforgivable, was that he'd done it without consulting Ryan. He'd talked to Dawn's dad about Ryan, but hadn't asked his permission first.

His chest hurt as he heaved for air, but it was nothing to the ache deep inside him. He'd ruined the best thing he'd ever had, but even worse than that was the expression on Ryan's face in the instant before fury had kicked in—a look that spoke of confusion and devastation as he'd stared at Sam.

Sam knew he was a loser, but he'd never known just how much until he'd seen the look of betrayal on Ryan's face and known that he'd caused it.

RYAN

Ryan spent the night packing. That, and building a pile of crap in the middle of the living room that was going in a skip just as soon as one could be delivered. The first thing in the pile was that watercolour of Bessie he'd bought. It had no artistic merit. No resale value.

Packing kept him away from the bottle of single malt in the kitchen and thoughts of how just one glass wouldn't hurt. He knew if he gave in to it, it would be the end to everything he'd tried to do differently here.

As the sky began to lighten, Ryan found his determination to leave had been replaced by a stubbornness deep inside. It was the same kind of stubborn that had led him to do stupid shit just because his father would disapprove, which meant it was probably a bloody awful idea, but he was determined not to make it easy for that bastard Cleaver. If he wanted to get rid of Ryan, he'd have to go the legitimate route and obey employment law, and the one thing he *couldn't* fire him for was his criminal record because he'd damn well declared it when he'd applied for the job. Cleaver held all the cards, but Ryan would make him play them down to the very last one rather than run away.

He got changed for work and headed out earlier than usual. That way he'd at least avoid the girl in the ticket office who always eyed him like he was a side of prime beef. The shrilling inside him eased when he greeted Bessie with a slap on her metalwork, cold in the early morning air. She didn't change. What she'd seen over so many years didn't bear thinking about—triumph and tragedy, and still the world went on.

When Simon arrived he looked at Ryan sharply, but said nothing beyond the usual "How's she doing this morning?"

All of it steadied Ryan. He might not be able to control losing Bessie, losing *this*, but the rest of it was up to him. Yeah, he could go back to that kid he'd been, that angry, miserable, fucked-up kid who hated the world, which hated him right back, or he could carry on down the new path he'd started along. It had its problems but it had given him something he'd never had before. He'd actually been happy, specially the last few weeks.

Somehow thoughts of messy, dark hair and excited eyes came to mind, but he pushed them away. He was leaving, moving on. Sam Chancellor had been a way to pass the time. Given what the moron had ended up doing it had been a fucking bad choice, but Ryan knew more than most about living with his choices.

He turned his attention back to Bessie. If today was the last day he got to spend with her, he'd make damn sure he enjoyed every minute.

SAM

Sam's eyes were sore and his nose blocked when he woke up. His stomach felt like it had been hollowed out, and for an instant he couldn't remember why. And then he wished he could forget.

He got up, unable to spend another minute in the bed he'd shared for so many nights with Ryan. And it was *typical* of his life that the one day he wanted to go to work and be distracted was his day off. At least escorting Mabel outside and having breakfast gave him a few moments respite, with his mind having to concentrate on other things, like the fact he was nearly out of Marmite. Not that Ryan had ever touched the stuff. That yawning pit in his stomach opened back up and he leaned over the sink, clutching at the edge of it as he breathed deeply to control the sick feeling inside him.

He couldn't do this. He had to try and make it right. Ryan would never forgive him—how could he?—but if he could just understand that Sam hadn't meant to do it, then maybe Sam would be able to breathe properly again. Leaving the toast in the toaster, he was out of the house before he had time to talk himself out of it.

The walk to the station, usually one of such anticipation, felt as if he was going to his execution. Thankfully Val was too busy serving customers to chat to him, because he didn't think he could cope with anyone right now. She merely waved at him, causing everyone in the queue to turn around and look as he trudged past.

His nerve almost failed him halfway across the footbridge to Platform 5. He hesitated, and stood on the bridge for a while, looking for Ryan. He knew Thursdays were Bess's maintenance day, so Ryan would be coming and going to the staffroom for cups of tea. He was ashamed of the relief he felt when there was no sign of him. And then it hit him—maybe Ryan wasn't here because he'd already been sacked. If so, he'd leave Cardale and Sam would never see him again, and Ryan would never get to know just how sorry he was.

He hurtled down the steps, desperate to see if Ryan was there, but all he could see was Bess, steaming her stately way from the water tank. There were no passengers on a Thursday—she must be going out on a test run. As she puffed past, with no reason to stop at the platform, he saw it *was* Ryan driving her. He was concentrating ferociously on the array of controls in front of him, and Sam had no idea if Ryan had even seen him. But it didn't matter. Ryan was still here. Sam would wait until Bess came back.

In the meantime, he found a little comfort in watching her steam past, her brass and paintwork shining and the windows of her carriages glinting in the sun. She was beautiful, every last part of her. She made even the most mundane, functional parts look graceful. Except...

He frowned because something marred those elegant clean lines at the end of the first carriage. Something was wrong, but he didn't realise what it was until the next carriage passed him. The angle cock on the brake pipe had been closed.

Jesus *Christ*, she had no brakes.

"*Ryan*!" He ran after Bess as fast as he could, yelling at the top of his voice and waving his arms wildly to try and get Ryan's attention, but it was no good—she was picking up speed and had already cleared the end of the platform. Ryan would be looking ahead of him, and he'd never hear anything above the sound of Bess.

Sam came to a panting, helpless halt at the end of the platform and watched her steam away. Sick terror gripped him. He didn't know what to do. There had to be someone—Marlene. She'd know what to do. He was halfway down the platform before he remembered the shop didn't open on a Thursday.

He froze, and all he could think was that Bess was going to crash and Ryan would be—oh God, *no*.

He spun around and raced up the steps, across the footbridge, because there wasn't anyone to tell. There was only one way to stop this. He had to get to the level section at the top of her climb from the valley and flag her down and hope to God that her engine brakes would be enough to hold the whole train. Once she started on the descent, it would be too late—without brakes on any of the carriages, she'd gather so much speed on the long way down that there was no way she'd stay on the track when she hit the sharp curve at the bottom. Oh *God*. He *had* to get to the top of the hill.

He ran desperately along the corridor, cursing as he dodged people coming the other way, and terror churned his stomach as he realised—he didn't have enough time to go home and get his car. By the time he got to the track, Bess would have gone down the hillside and derailed. God, if she did that, her boiler would blow and there'd be nothing left. Nothing of Bess, and nothing of Ryan.

Somehow his brain kept working through the horror of it, and he dodged into the ticket office. "Your car," he gabbled at Val as he barged some guy out of the way. "I need to borrow it. Now, Val, *please.*"

Val's mouth hung open as she stared at him, and Sam had no idea what she saw, whether the desperation he felt was reflected on his face. "It's Bess—I have to stop her before she crashes. *Now.*"

He had no idea why, but Val was reaching into the handbag on her desk and passing the keys through the slot where she usually doled out tickets.

"If you so much as scratch it—" she started.

He didn't hear the rest of it. He didn't even thank her. He just snatched the keys and *ran*.

He wasted a precious five seconds trying to get the seat back far enough to accommodate the difference between Val's leg-length and his, and then he was peeling out of the staff car park and speeding out of town.

He knew exactly how long Bess took on each part of her daily route, and if he took the single-track road that acted as a short cut, he'd be able to do it. Just so long as long as he didn't meet anything coming the other way, forcing one of them to reverse for miles.

He lost valuable seconds agonising when he reached the turn-off. If he went this way and met another vehicle, it was over. But if he took the long way round, he might not make it in time to stop her.

He sobbed a desperate breath and turned the car down the narrow, potholed lane. And then he couldn't do anything except put his foot down and pray.

Chapter Thirteen

SAM

Sam had lived this nightmare before, where he was running and it wasn't fast enough to stop whatever terrible thing was going to happen. But this time he knew what the terrible thing was, and he knew he was awake. He gasped for air as he pushed himself on across the field, towards the railway line. He couldn't let this happen—Ryan *couldn't* die.

He reached the track as a plume of smoke above the trees announced Bess was about to round the curve onto the section of line where he was waiting. His fingers clenched on the silver windscreen sunshade he'd grabbed from Val's car and he thanked God it was a sunny day—surely Ryan couldn't miss seeing something that size if he waved it.

But what if he *did*? What if he thought Sam was just somebody waving at Bess the way everyone did when she went past? Or maybe he'd see it was Sam and he'd speed up to get past him even faster.

There was only one way to prevent that.

He swallowed hard as he stepped onto the track. It went against *everything* he'd been taught, over and over. One of those safety videos Uncle Ken had made him watch still haunted him sometimes—kids playing chicken with a train, until one of them jumped out of the way at the last minute only for his foot to slip and get wedged under the rail. It had given him nightmares for months afterwards, thinking about that kid's leg getting sliced off. At least Uncle Ken had stopped showing him the videos after that. But Sam couldn't think about all the things that could go wrong. He had to do this. He *had* to stop Bess.

The sunshade wasn't going to be enough. He pulled his T-shirt over his head and held it in his other hand. Then he waited and tried to remember how to breathe.

RYAN

Ryan was leaning forward slightly as he nursed Bessie up the last bit of the lengthy, zig-zagging climb, straightening when they came out onto the top. This was his favourite part of the loop, so high up and open that it felt like the roof of the world for those few minutes before they started back down into the valley. It was partly the view he loved, and partly the way he could swear Bessie relaxed once they gained level ground after that punishing long climb.

He was looking around at the rolling green hillsides, so restful and peaceful—apart from the unholy din Bessie always made—and trying not to think that this was probably the last time he'd see this view, when something glinted in the sun ahead of him. He screwed his eyes up to see better in the glare that was bouncing off whatever it was.

Shit! He tugged on the whistle, three short, sharp bursts, warning whatever idiot was standing there half-naked on the railway line to get out of the damn way. But the bloke just stood there, waving wildly. Either he was a certifiable lunatic, in which case the last thing Ryan was going to do was stop the train because he'd probably hack him and Simon to death with an axe before stealing Bessie, or there was a problem with the line up ahead.

"*Ryan!*" Simon had seen him too, just as Ryan decided possible axe mutilation was a better option than getting in a train crash and slammed Bessie's brake into the emergency position. Instead of the abrupt deceleration that usually caused, there was a screeching of wheels, a juddering that shook her from stem to stern, and Bessie ploughed on, a hundred tons of steel and power.

He released the brake and tried again. Nothing happened.

As it failed a third time, it finally dawned on him that it didn't matter how many times he tried, it wasn't going to work. Panic churned his gut, but he forced it down, forced himself to *think*.

He reached for the steam brake, the one that was designed to brake only Bessie, not the rest of the train. Simon's gaze was glued to his face, but he was mercifully silent as Ryan wrapped his hand around the old metal lever and drew a deep breath.

He was taking their lives in his hands, literally. If he opened this too quickly, her wheels would lock and the momentum of the carriages behind her would push her on, over the edge of the hill. If he was too cautious, too slow, they wouldn't stop in time. Either way, all that would be left was a plunge down the steep hillside ending in a tangle of twisted steel and scalding steam. He'd tell Simon to jump if it came to that.

Straining to listen to what Bessie was telling him, he started to open the valve, his gaze fixed on the rails ahead of him, calculating how much further they had before everything went to hell. As

Bessie ate up the yards at a terrifying speed, he realised who was on the track before them waving like a madman. Sam Chancellor was standing full square in Bessie's way as she powered relentlessly towards him.

"*Get off the fucking line!*" Ryan screamed it, his fear finding voice in rage. Of course Sam didn't hear, and he stayed exactly where he was, right in Bessie's path.

Simon was hanging out of the side of the cab, gesturing and yelling at Sam to get out of the way, but his words were torn away by Bessie's slipstream.

To his shame, Ryan closed his eyes. He didn't want to see it—he couldn't *bear* to see Sam, so courageous and defiant as he tried to warn them something was wrong, dying beneath the wheels of the engine he loved.

SAM

At first Sam thought Ryan hadn't seen him, but then he heard the brakes squealing and saw the way Bess was juddering. He kept waving, because it seemed like the only thing he could do to help whatever frantic efforts Ryan and Simon were making. He waved his shirt and the big sheet of silver plastic above his head like they could stop Bess, and all the time he was chanting, "*Please, please, please.*"

She was suddenly bearing down on him with terrifying speed, huge and powerful. She'd plough through him as if he wasn't even there. He waved his arms frantically over his head one last time, then turned and leaped off the track.

She was close enough that he swore he felt the heat from her boiler, but thank God there was no horrifying slip of the foot to betray him when he threw himself clear. He sprawled in the grass by the edge of the track as she thundered past, and his vision blurred because it hadn't worked. Bess was going to crash.

He couldn't watch, but he had to. As he blinked furiously to clear his eyes, he thought he must be imagining it, but then he realised it really was happening, that the locomotive brakes, still squealing like animals in distress, were beginning to hold. Ryan had seen him before she'd picked up all of her usual speed after the climb.

He couldn't breathe through the surge of hope that the brakes she *did* have might hold her. Even if they didn't stop her, if they only slowed her, then Ryan and Simon could jump to safety. The instant he thought it, he was up and sprinting after her, trying to catch up enough to yell to them to jump.

It wasn't just his imagination—he was catching up. She was definitely slowing. As he drew level with the last carriage, she finally came to a complete, shuddering halt, and the only sounds were the hiss of steam and Sam's ragged, terrified breathing.

"What the *fuck*?" Ryan leaped from the footplate, and seemed for an instant not to know whether to head straight for Sam or examine Bess. After glaring at Sam for a moment, his face white with fury, he turned his attention to Bess and saw almost straight away what Sam had spotted at the station.

"Simon, put the bloody carriage brakes on *now*," he snapped. "All of them."

Simon, who'd been following him, looking pale and shaken, ran to the nearest carriage.

Ryan turned his attention to Sam. "What the *fuck*?" he said again.

Ryan was livid. Everything in Sam told him to run, to stay safe, but he couldn't move. His legs were trembling and the shaking was spreading throughout his body as Ryan advanced on him, eyes hot and furious.

"You fucking *idiot.*" Ryan was in front of him. "You don't go on the fucking *line.*"

Sam wanted to tell Ryan he *knew* that, but he couldn't breathe. He was opening his mouth but nothing was coming out except strangled gasps for air. The race to stop Bess, the horror of thinking he'd failed and the memory of her bearing down on him at such terrifying speed were all mixed up in his head and he couldn't *think.*

"You fucking *moron.*"

He flinched as Ryan's hands grabbed at him, but then Ryan was folding him into his arms and holding him close, and he was warm and comforting and *alive.* Oh God, Ryan was *alive.* He clutched at his overalls and held on as tight as he could.

RYAN

Ryan had never felt such fury—he could have *killed* Sam, and all because the fucking idiot hadn't got out of the way in time. But when he saw Sam hunched in on himself, throat bobbing as he swallowed, those dark eyes huge with shock as Ryan blasted furious words at him, his temper faded as quickly as Bessie's smoke in the summer sky. He'd pulled Sam close, and jeez, he was trembling.

As Ryan held him, the familiar body pressed against his and Sam's head buried in his neck, his breathing rough and uneven against Ryan's skin, he found something deep inside himself wasn't quite steady either. It had been so close. Too fucking close.

He'd studied rail accidents as part of his training and he had no illusions what would have happened to him, Simon and Bessie if they'd started down that hill without brakes. But instead of the violent death that had been staring him in the face just seconds ago, he was standing in the sunshine, the faint sound of sheep bleating in the distance almost drowned by Sam's rough breathing. They'd made it.

His arms tightened until he thought he might break Sam's ribs, because Sam was here, alive and whole, and not a mangled mess beneath Bessie's wheels. God, Ryan had thought... But Sam was okay. They were *both* okay. As was the beautiful, stubborn old engine Sam had risked his life for.

"She's okay," Ryan said, because Sam's breathing was still uneven enough to worry him. "Bessie's okay."

Sam huffed what might have been a laugh but sounded more like a sob where his face was pressed against Ryan's neck. "It's not *her* I was worried about."

Ryan drew a sharp, shocked breath. It hurt his throat and his chest, and he was scared to let it out, in case it hurt as much on the return journey. But his heart was hammering and he had to breathe, damn it.

The next breath hurt a little less, though there was an unaccustomed ache deep in his throat. Because Sam—that crazy, stupid bastard had thrown himself in front of a speeding train for Ryan. With no hesitation and, apparently, no regrets. Ryan wasn't sure which of them was trembling now. He'd never known anything like the feelings tearing through him.

His hand wound in Sam's hair and held his face close against his neck, partly so he could feel him breathe and know he was still alive, and partly so Sam couldn't see his face. If he saw, he'd know just how close Ryan was to something he hadn't done—not sober, anyway—since his ninth birthday, when his dad had told him that the investment choices he'd made with such care and diligence for his birthday money were short-sighted and stupid. He swallowed hard as he held Sam, and the threatened tears slowly retreated.

Sam was speaking again. His words were muffled against Ryan's skin, but Ryan heard them. "I'm sorry," he was saying. "I'm so sorry. I never thought they'd print what they did. I was just trying to help."

Right now that bloody newspaper article was the last thing on Ryan's mind, but Sam was now so tense in his hold, it was obvious how much it mattered to him.

"I know," he said, rubbing his cheek against Sam's hair before he realised what he was doing and stopped himself. The next words were more difficult to force out, but the distress in Sam's voice made him want to make everything better. "If there'd been nothing for them to find, it wouldn't have mattered. I'm the one who did those things, not you."

Sam raised his head. "But if I hadn't—"

"Hey." The word was sharp, but Ryan's tone was soft. "After what nearly happened just now, I don't give a toss about it," he said, and kissed Sam. He wanted to taste every bit of Sam's mouth, to know he was here and safe. It seemed Sam was just as determined to do the same in return until their kiss was hot and deep and never going to end.

"Listen, mate, we need to do something about Bess."

Simon's voice had Ryan pulling back, though it took him a moment to focus on Simon's words. He felt as dazed as Sam looked right now. What had Simon said? Oh, yeah—Bessie.

"Give us ten minutes first?" he asked. He knew he couldn't risk driving her again until she'd undergone a full inspection. He also knew it would take most of the day and involve countless people and questions. They'd come so close to disaster that he wanted to be with Sam just a little longer before the word crashed in on them.

He wanted to be as close to him as he could get and to know that they were both alive.

"I already did, mate," Simon said, but he heaved a resigned sigh. "Just ten minutes, mind," he said. "I'm going to dump out the fire—it's not like she'll be going anywhere for a while. And you owe me, Saunders."

"Anything," Ryan promised fervently. That was a daft thing to say, because Simon would probably get him to clean out Bessie's ash pan from here until eternity, but he didn't care because Sam was in his arms, kissing him again. Hard and deep, on and on.

"God, Sam," he said at last, pulling back. Sam's eyes were dark and dazed, his bare chest was rising and falling unevenly, and Ryan *wanted*. With a need that hurt, he wanted to be as close to him as possible.

They lay down together on the springy turf, and Ryan loved that Sam didn't worry about Simon, about modesty, or anything except touching Ryan, holding him as close as he could. They kept kissing, and if he didn't stop kissing Sam sometime soon, their ten minutes would be up and they wouldn't have done anything more than kiss.

Reluctantly, he relinquished Sam's mouth, loving the little sound of disappointed protest Sam made as he did so. He closed his lips around Sam's nipple instead, using tongue and then the slight scrape of teeth, and Sam was bucking up under him, swearing. Ryan pulled off, puffed a sharp breath across the wet peak of Sam's nipple, and as Sam swore again, he took the opportunity to slide his hand down Sam's stomach and into his jeans. Sam was suddenly still and silent, because Ryan's hand was on the hot, impossibly hard line of his cock through the thin cotton of his boxers.

Ryan didn't waste any more time. He had Sam's jeans open, Sam raising his hips to help him work them down to mid-thigh and reveal Sam's cock, big and ready for him. He needed it in his mouth.

Sam was clutching at the grass beneath him, fingers tearing into the turf as Ryan worked his head up and down, getting into a rhythm that had Sam gasping and writhing. He wasn't the only one. Ryan was practically humping the ground, it felt so good having Sam like this, but he couldn't take the time to negotiate his overalls and then his jeans—he'd sort himself out later. This was for Sam.

No, this was for both of them, he realised, as with a garbled shout that Simon—not to mention half of Cardale—must have heard, Sam came.

Ryan stayed still for a few moments afterwards, breathing deeply to calm himself down because his dick felt like it might go off with just the friction of his jeans if he moved and he was *not* spending the next however many hours out here with spunk in his jeans like a fricking teenager. When he thought it was finally safe to move, he flopped down beside Sam, who was still breathing hard and whose smile at Ryan was as bright as the sun.

Sam turned onto his side and reached out to the zipper of Ryan's overalls. Ryan snagged his hand before it could get anywhere too interesting. "Later," he said, and it sounded like a promise.

As they lay there grinning idiotically at one another, larks singing overhead and the scent of hawthorn blossom softening the air around them, Ryan knew his promise had been heard and understood.

Chapter Fourteen

SAM

By the time Simon ventured warily from the shelter of Bessie's footplate, Sam was decent again. He couldn't stop grinning at Ryan, who was returning his smile, his eyes crinkled at the corners in the way Sam loved. *This* was Ryan, not the terrible person the newspaper had said he was. Sam accepted that he'd done all those things, but it wasn't *who* he was. When Ryan crouched down to get a better look at the angle cock, though, the smile was wiped from his face as if it had never been.

"I inspected her before we left, I know I did." He looked at Simon, "You *saw* me. I'd never have missed this."

"I know you wouldn't, mate," Simon said. "Which means this must have been done on purpose when we were in the cab."

The world whirled around Sam. "Someone *did* this to Bess? But *who*? And *why*?"

Ryan put up a hand and Sam obediently closed his mouth to hold back the torrent of words trying to get out. "How did you know?" Ryan asked. "And how the hell did you get out here? You were still at the station when we left."

"I saw the angle cock was closed when she went past," Sam said. "I tried to make you hear, but you were past the end of the platform. So I borrowed Val's car."

"Val?"

"The tarty girl from the ticket office," Simon said.

Sam frowned. "She's not tarty. She's nice. And by the way, she just saved your life."

Simon barked a surprised-sounding laugh. "Fair enough."

"But *who*—" Sam started again.

"Not our job to guess," Ryan said to him, with a swift, meaningful glance in Simon's direction. Sam took the warning and shut up. "We'll have to let the station know. I guess we should tell the Old Bill, because they might need to set up some sort of security while she's stranded up here. And the rail accident board are going to need to know, even if it wasn't strictly an accident. I don't suppose you have their number in your phone?" he asked Sam.

Sam stared at him. "Why on earth would I?"

"Because it's to do with trains," Ryan said, as if it was obvious. "Never mind, I'll Google it." He held out a hand, and Sam dug his phone out of his pocket and passed it over. "We should get Perkins from the maintenance company out here too."

Simon groaned. "God, Saunders—near-death experiences and outdoor sex aren't enough for one day? You have to get that dickhead involved too?"

"He's thorough," Ryan said, not raising his gaze from where he was typing something into Sam's phone.

"That's one word for it," Simon said glumly.

RYAN

They didn't leave until Bessie was in safe hands, with a whole heap of people milling around her. They included Perkins, a couple of policewomen and the head of the board of trustees, who'd shown up with his wife, three grandchildren and two excited black Labradors. Apparently they'd been out walking when he got the call and he'd piled everyone in the car and come straight over.

Ryan, Simon and Sam went over what had happened multiple times for their different audiences. The disbelieving eyebrow that one of the policewomen raised on hearing Sam's story of spotting the problem as Bessie went past him lowered pretty quickly when he misunderstood it as a request for more information and launched into an explanation of train brakes.

"...because the vacuum system requires much larger actuators and consumes more energy," he'd been explaining when Ryan joined them.

"So you saw the cock was turned off," she said, evidently trying to get him to move on to what had happened next. Instead, Sam had nodded eagerly and plunged on to educate her about why the failsafe on the vacuum system that would have prevented Bess moving with disabled brakes didn't work on this type of air brake system. Ryan had tried desperately not to smirk too obviously. God bless Sam Chancellor and his enthusiasm.

In the midst of all this, the police had called the fire brigade to cut through the fence between the road and the field in which Bess was standing, to allow easy access to everyone who needed to inspect her. That had kept Ryan happy for a while. He might have a bit of a fireman fetish, but who didn't?

The firemen had only just left when the guy from the rail accident investigation board showed up. Once he had taken preliminary statements from Ryan, Simon and Sam, he told them they were free to go. Before they did, Ryan took Sam's phone again and made one last call. To Cleaver.

He knew he should have called him first, but he was also aware Cleaver would blame him for not spotting the fault. He *knew* he'd checked her brakes. The only way this could have happened was if, as Simon had said, someone had done this on purpose. The way Simon hadn't doubted him for an instant had warmed his heart, but it wouldn't help him when Cleaver heard. He'd be sacked on the spot.

The other reason he hadn't called Cleaver before now was a nagging suspicion that wouldn't leave him alone. He couldn't *really* believe that Cleaver would have done this, but there was no doubting that Bessie would attract a hell of an insurance payout. Maybe Cleaver had got spooked by Sam contacting the newspaper with gossip about the trust being in financial trouble and wanted to get out while he could, with one last fat cheque.

And if Cleaver really *was* behind this and had done something more than turn the angle cock, the accident board guy and Perkins had had full access to Bessie before Cleaver had been able to stop them. Those two seemed to be a match made in heaven, conferring intently about minuscule measurements and worn flanges.

His gut unclenched in relief when he got voicemail. He left a brief message telling Cleaver there'd been a problem with Bess, who was currently stranded on the top of the hill, and that the head of the trustees, Dr Matthews, was with her.

"Will she be okay out here?" Sam asked as Ryan gave him the phone back. "No one's going to come and vandalise her, are they?"

"Matthews said he'd arrange for a couple of people to stay with her until she's been declared safe to drive back to the station," Ryan said. Matthews had said that while regarding Ryan with undisguised disgust, though Ryan couldn't tell if it was because of the newspaper story or because he thought the whole incident was Ryan's fault.

Simon came with them back to town, which put paid to any discussion about Cleaver during the journey. It also made the cherry-red Mini feel even more like a toy car than it looked, having three big men squashed into it. Sam's knees were practically up round his ears as he drove.

As Ryan watched him, those large hands so steady and confident on the gear stick and steering wheel, something twisted inside him and he had to look away, staring out of the window as the houses they were passing blurred slightly.

Back at the station, Simon and Ryan retrieved their belongings from their lockers, having unanimously volunteered Sam to return Val's keys. Ryan felt a bit mean about it. For approximately half a second, until he remembered the way Val tended to look at him—as if she wanted to do unspeakable things to him. He still wasn't sure if they were of a sexual nature or something a little more homicidal. He couldn't understand how shy, socially awkward Sam knew her. In the circumstances, he was simply grateful he did.

Parting ways from Simon outside the station, he found Sam waiting for him. A delighted smile opened his face when he saw Ryan. All sorts of instincts were firing, warning Ryan that this was dangerous, but a deeper intuition overrode them all and he smiled back at Sam, wider than he could remember smiling in a lifetime.

SAM

The subject he wanted to talk to Ryan about—who could have sabotaged Bess—faded into insignificance when Ryan looked at him, *saw* him, and smiled like that, happy and open. There'd been a softness to Ryan he'd never known before, up on that hillside, and Sam wanted to revel in it without any distractions. And perhaps Ryan felt the same, because they walked back to Sam's in silence. It wasn't awkward. It was almost as if what lay between them was too important for words.

Or maybe, Sam realised as he unlocked the front door and Ryan yawned behind him, Ryan was just tired after the events of the day.

"Sorry," Ryan said. "I didn't sleep last night."

"You realise you don't need to be subtle to get into my bed, don't you?" Sam said.

It earned him a glinting grin from Ryan and ended up with him flat on his back in his bed, naked, with an equally naked Ryan driving him crazy. Because Ryan didn't seem like he was going to screw Sam anytime soon. He was instead exploring every part of Sam's body with his mouth.

Including, most especially, his hipbones. Sam had never thought of them as an erogenous zone, but Ryan seemed fascinated by them, coming back to them over and over again, following their lines with his tongue and sucking dark marks into the thin skin until Sam was squirming under him.

"*Please,*" he said, which he'd been saying for the last lifetime at least, but at *last* Ryan seemed to hear how desperate he was, because he reached out for the lube. When he returned his attention to Sam's other hipbone, he slid a finger deep inside him. Sam groaned, because it felt so damn good, but he wanted more. He wanted Ryan's thick cock to open him and fill him.

And thank *God* Ryan seemed finally to be of the same mind because he had another finger inside Sam, working him in a rhythm that had Sam's hips rising and falling as he begged shamelessly for Ryan's cock. By the time Ryan had rolled on a condom and pressed in, Sam was beyond words. He was beyond anything except the feel of Ryan, giving him everything he'd ever wanted.

He clutched at Ryan's arms where he was braced over Sam, then wrapped his hand in his hair and dragged him down for an out-of-control, open-mouthed kiss as Ryan kept fucking into him, slow and maddening. Sam held him there, sharing breaths as Ryan's control broke and the long, slow strokes were gone and Ryan was bucking into him, little high-pitched noises escaping him as he thrust fully home each time until he was shuddering, pulsing out his climax. When Sam reached down a hand to bring himself off, Ryan stopped him. The very first touch of Ryan's hand on his cock had Sam crying out and wetness stringing over him. And then they were pressed so close together they felt like part of one another.

RYAN

Ryan stirred, becoming aware of Sam's warm body tangled up with him and soft breaths on his shoulder. He reluctantly opened his eyes, part of him not wanting this to end. Sam's leg was thrown over his, and he was snuggled into Ryan, but not in a possessive, claiming way. It was more like an honest, wanting to be as close as he possibly could way.

Maybe Ryan was fooling himself, but he didn't think so. He'd never known anyone quite like Sam Chancellor, and he was coming to realise just how many surprises lay beneath that apparently meek and shy surface.

Ryan slowly disentangled himself from Sam's grasp. Nice as this was, he knew it would be a lot less nice tomorrow morning, what with dried spunk and sweat, not to mention the inevitable oil and grease that had worked their way somehow inside his overalls. They'd better clean up before they ended up stuck together, and not in a sexy way.

Sam stirred. "What time is it?" It was a very definite grumble.

"10 p.m.," Ryan said. "So don't give me that 'don't do mornings' crap."

Sam's lips curved into the beginnings of a smile, though his eyes remained resolutely closed against the orange of the streetlights through the bedroom window. "I must have fallen asleep," he said.

"How do you do it, Mr Holmes?" Ryan marvelled. He threw back the duvet, which they'd retained just enough sense to crawl under earlier before falling fast asleep, and sat on the edge of the bed. "I need a shower."

"You do that," Sam said, and drew the duvet over his head.

"Oh no you don't." Ryan yanked the duvet off him, leaving Sam staring at him, wide-eyed with betrayal and sporting the worst case of bedhead Ryan had ever seen. Seriously, the guy could audition for a scarecrow and be told he was an overachiever. "You need to go big-game hunting before I can shower."

"Mabel never shows up before about 2 a.m.," Sam said, reaching blindly for a duvet that was no longer there. "Damn it," he said, looking at Ryan. "I'm awake now."

His petulant little pout was the most endearing thing Ryan had ever seen. As he leaned in and kissed him, he realised he was possibly losing his mind, because there was no way on earth petulance could be attractive.

"Up," he said, fingers going unerringly to Sam's ticklish spot. "You need to shower too."

He was nearly brained by Sam whiplashing off the bed in response to his fingers. It probably served him right, though he wasn't above playing up his injury enough that Sam accompanied him into the shower.

Ryan carefully spread shower gel over Sam's broad shoulders and down the smooth skin of his back, filled with awareness of what he had almost lost today. And somehow touching Sam like that felt more intimate than any sex Ryan had ever had.

SAM

"Tell me you've got food," Ryan said as he flicked the kettle on. "I'm starving."

Sam's stomach had been grumbling as they'd dried off after the shower and his mind had already been turning over what he had in the house. "Bacon butties?"

The speed with which Ryan grabbed the loaf of bread and started slicing it was answer enough.

Five minutes later they took generously filled butties and mugs of tea through to the sitting room. Sam was wearing Uncle Ken's old dressing gown and had lent Ryan his towelling robe. He couldn't work out how Ryan made even a functional, shapeless garment look good.

"You haven't been on your train chatroom," Ryan said, nodding towards the laptop on the floor as Sam swallowed the final mouthful of his butty. It wasn't his fault he'd guzzled it before Ryan was halfway through his. He'd been hungry and it had tasted good. "I'd have thought you couldn't wait to tell them about waving Bess down with your underwear before fainting gracefully in front of her."

"You're getting real life confused with *The Railway Children*," Sam chided. "And it wasn't their underwear they waved—it was red flannel petticoats."

"I knew it." Ryan's grin stretched from ear to ear. "I knew you were a *Railway Children* fan."

It wasn't as if he could deny that he and Uncle Ken had watched it every Christmas Day for years. Sam always got choked up at the end, even though they'd only watched it for the locomotives because one of them had come from the same works that produced Bess.

With a start, he realised he hadn't thought of Bess for hours, sitting still and silent out there in the dark countryside.

RYAN

"What's going to happen now?" Sam asked as Ryan finished his sandwich, licking his fingers to make sure he hadn't missed any melted butter. "I mean, they'll mend Bess and she'll just keep running, won't she?"

Ryan put his plate down on the arm of the sofa and leaned back beside Sam, gloom descending on him at the thought of the investigation into what had happened and what it would mean for him. "People might not want to ride on her after this—they might think it could happen again."

"But they'll know Cleaver did it, so once he's arrested, there won't be any problem, surely."

"You think Cleaver did it?"

"Well, yeah," Sam said, as if it was obvious. "Don't you?"

"What I think and what can be proved are two different things," Ryan said. "No one would have thought twice if they'd seen him inspecting Bessie's couplings because he's the sort of dickhead who never trusts that anyone can do their job properly. So he has immediate plausible deniability"—another of his father's catchphrases—"not to mention that the guy who mugged me nicked my keys. Engine shed, staffroom, the works. Whoever he was, he could have been lurking around the place for all we know, getting in where he shouldn't."

Sam's mouth fell open and he stared at Ryan. "I hadn't thought of that." That was fair enough. It had only occurred to Ryan when he'd been buttering the bread for the butties. "But you do think it was Cleaver, don't you?"

"'Course it was," Ryan said. "That so-called mugging is proof. Why the hell would any self-respecting mugger pick on someone who should have been able to fight back?" He caught himself picking at the loose thread on the pocket of the robe in his embarrassment that he'd made no effort to defend himself. "No, it was a setup to make it look like anyone could have had access, which means it's someone who *does* have legitimate access. And of those people, there's only one suspect." Maybe that logic wouldn't stand up to scrutiny, but he knew he was right. "Cleaver saw the noose closing in on him when you went to the paper and he took the chance for one final huge payout. He was going to pocket that insurance cheque and take himself off somewhere the law couldn't touch him. What he's been taking has been peanuts compared to what he'd get for Bess, and there'd probably be some sort of insurance on me and Simon as well, as employees."

Sam sat up straight, his nostrils quivering. "But that's—that's—" His voice cracked with his strength of feeling. "He *couldn't*."

Ryan couldn't remember ever being as innocent and trusting as Sam. "Money talks," he said, and hated that he was quoting his father. That thought brought another, unwelcome revelation. "Oh *shit*."

"What?" Sam asked in alarm.

"I'd better warn my father if the Old Bill's going to go poking around in the accounts. They might want to know why he made a sizeable donation just after I got taken on."

Sam's mouth was open. "He did?"

"There's nothing untowards about it," Ryan said. "He merely became aware of the sterling work of the trust after I got the job and decided to support it."

Sam was still looking decidedly shocked. He also looked upset, as if Ryan had disappointed him. Unaccountably, that stung.

"Your dad paid for you to get the job?" Sam asked.

"Only if you want to see it that way," Ryan said, then shook his head. Fuck. Sam might as well know everything about him. It stood to reason the only reason Sam lit up like he did whenever he saw Ryan was because he didn't know the real him. "Yeah, my father bribed Cleaver to get me the job," he said. "He also bought me the flat, on condition we went our separate ways so I never embarrassed him again. And all that crap in the paper? It was true, just so you know."

Sam nodded slightly. "I thought it must have been, or your father would have sued them for libel."

It was calm and accepting, and unlike any reaction Ryan was used to. He didn't know what to say.

"Look, it's in the past," Sam said. "The guy I know is good and kind—" He glared slightly at Ryan's scornful snort. "And cares about Bess."

"Because that's the most important mark of character in your book," Ryan said. He'd had to say *something* through the tightness in his throat.

"It's true."

"It's not all of the truth." Ryan couldn't understand why the hell he was making Sam face the ugliness of who he was. He supposed that otherwise he'd be living a lie, some sort of fantasy with Sam thinking he was something he wasn't. "I was an arrogant, spoiled, angry little shit for years," he said. "No excuses for what I did. I did it because I could. Because I wanted to."

"What changed?" Sam asked.

Ryan barked out a sound that might have been a laugh. Sam's question wasn't in the least bit funny, but it was the last thing he'd expected. None of the disgust or the prurience he was used to. Just a simple, important question that was so very far from simple to answer.

"I don't know," he said honestly. He found himself picking at that damn loose thread again. "I just woke up one morning, hungover, with no idea what the hell I'd done the previous night, and didn't want to do that any more. There was no big revelation or anything. Hell, I had to see a shrink as part of my probation terms, and even he never got me to see anything differently, though maybe that was because he was fixated on the delusion that I had daddy issues."

The contempt he felt for that diagnosis caused his throat to tighten, and he swallowed.

"I didn't hurt anyone, though," he said, needing Sam to know. "A few of us got trashed one night at a club and when the bouncers tried to get us to leave, we kind of ran wild. Like '70s rock stars or something, chucking stuff through windows, smashing all the bottles and glasses behind the bar, that kind of crap. And normally we'd have just been fined, but the judge thought she should make an example of kids who'd done that after growing up with 'every advantage', and so I got sent down for a few weeks. But I didn't hurt anyone." He didn't know why it was so important for Sam to understand that, but it was.

"The paper said something about an assault charge?" Sam's voice was so neutral he might as well have been Swiss.

"Yeah, that was about the one thing I *didn't* do." Ryan said. "This paparazzi dickhead kept sticking his camera in my face and when he did it one time too many I shoved it away. It hit him in the face, and he tried to get me done for assault. All he wanted was a story and that's how the coppers saw it too, because they dropped the case."

"I hope they did him for wasting police time," Sam said venomously, and Ryan couldn't help it—he laughed. Sam had heard the whole litany of ugliness and *that* was what he came out with.

And then Sam sat and simply drank his tea, seemingly not wanting to poke about in the ruins of Ryan's life. He was the first person who hadn't. The tension began to bleed out of Ryan's body and he picked up his own mug of tea. He'd been given the *Mallard* mug again, and he had the feeling that was a sacrifice on Sam's part. But that was Sam all over—so easily generous, yet the furthest thing from a pushover Ryan could imagine.

"I'd better phone Melanie tomorrow and tell her I won't be in to work," Sam said after a while. The police wanted to see Ryan at nine, with Sam straight after, and the accident board people wanted to see them at midday.

Ryan wished they weren't so efficient. He'd rather have waited a few days, because it was pretty obvious what their verdict was going to be after he'd taken a train out that had a clearly visible fault.

If he'd had any doubts, they'd vanished when he'd had to hand back his keys to the disapproving trustee guy who could scarcely bring himself to touch them after Ryan had. He'd told Ryan that they'd get a relief driver to take Bess back to the station when she was declared safe to be moved. There was no doubt that Ryan was going to be out of a job at the end of tomorrow, but worse than that—he'd probably never be allowed to drive another locomotive. Maybe it was karma for all the things he'd done over the years.

"More tea?"

But as he looked up at Sam standing in front of him, his eyes warm as he offered Ryan something for nothing, losing the job he'd come to love no longer seemed to be the end of the world.

SAM

Being interviewed by the police was nothing like Sam had imagined. He'd assumed that he would simply tell them his side of what had happened. Instead, by the time he reeled out of the small interview room, he'd spent nearly an hour answering the same questions over and over again from two middle-aged men who'd been perfectly polite but who had looked at him with hard eyes and kept asking him to clarify things. And the more they did that, the more he stumbled in his answers and said more than he'd intended to. In response to the question of whether he'd ever been in the engine shed, he'd not only confessed that yes, he had, and had touched Bess, but also that he and Ryan had ended up having sex in the staffroom afterwards. He was so unsettled by that point that he probably gave them a blow-by-blow account of exactly what he and Ryan had done.

Relief swamped him as he finally escaped, walking out of the building and into the freedom of the overcast morning. Ryan's voice calling his name made him jump.

"Am I glad to see you," Sam blurted out as Ryan straightened up from the wall he'd been slouching against. Ryan had been interviewed before him, and *his* interview had lasted nearly two hours. Sam thought he would have been long gone. "They think I did it."

Ryan laughed slightly, but it wasn't mocking. If anything, it sounded sympathetic. "That's what they do," he said. "If you'd been in a coma in Antarctica for the last six years, they'd still convince you that you're a suspect. That way the people who are guilty give up more than they know."

"But I didn't do—"

"They know that," Ryan said. "Come on, Sam, look at you. If someone gave you too much change in a shop, you'd go back and tell them. They can see that in you, don't worry."

The knots of unease in his stomach began to unclench, and he was able to smile at Ryan. "So how was your interview?"

"I told them about the dodgy accounts and that Cleaver threatened my job, claiming impending financial ruin," Ryan said. "Didn't tell them our theory, of course—they don't want suspects theorising, just the facts. But even a bunch of country coppers should be able to put it together."

He didn't sound too convinced, though, so Sam sought to change the subject. He was *sure* the police would sort it out, but he also got the feeling that Ryan would never agree with him on that. "Thanks for waiting for me," he said.

"Figured you might need some moral support. We're out of the frying pan and into the fire, anyway—we have to see the accident board next."

Sam frowned. "But the accident board just want to know what happened," he said. "Not like the police, who want to know who did it."

"They're the ones who'll take my licence away," Ryan said harshly. "I swear I did the visual inspection, but there's no doubt the brake was turned off. The answer's obvious—either I wasn't paying attention or I didn't do the check at all."

"But you're *good* at your job," Sam protested. "You care about Bess. Of course you'd have seen it if there was anything to see. Simon must be right—someone did it when you'd already finished your inspection."

"And if they believe that, they'll swallow the one about the unicorn who sleeps in the tender," Ryan said. Despite his mocking words, his voice had lost its brittle edge. "Come on, then. We might as well get it over with."

Despite the reason for walking with Ryan through the centre of town in the middle of the day, Sam couldn't help but feel that this was how things should be. It felt so easy, so natural to be with him like this. He refused to believe the accident board would see Ryan as anything other than the amazing driver he was, and the police would realise Cleaver was behind everything. Everything would be okay. He just knew it.

RYAN

Ryan sat on a chair outside the station manager's office, which had been commandeered for the morning. Simon had come out as they'd arrived. He'd grimaced at Ryan, but said nothing. Not that Simon usually said much, but his silence spoke volumes in this situation.

Sam had gone in first. As the minutes crawled past, Ryan got more and more edgy. There was an unexpected burst of laughter from the office behind him, and while he was still straining his ears to see if he could hear anything more, Sam emerged, looking happy and relaxed, the exact opposite of how he'd looked coming out of the police station. It figured. It had doubtless been a solid twenty minutes of talking about trains. Pretty much Sam's definition of heaven.

"I'll wait for you here," Sam said as Ryan got slowly to his feet. Although he knew it would change nothing that happened in that room, somehow it helped to know Sam was here, waiting for him, caring about the outcome.

Ryan squared his shoulders and, head held high, walked into the room where his future would be decided.

Chapter Fifteen

RYAN

"I told you," Sam enthused for about the forty-sixth time on the way back to his house. "I *told* you they'd see what a brilliant job you did in stopping her. I bet most drivers wouldn't have been able to."

The questioning from the three men who constituted the panel had been exhaustive, but Ryan had managed to keep calm for Bessie's sake. They needed to understand that it must have been sabotage in order to protect her from anything else that might happen. And eventually, when Ryan's shirt was sticking to his back with nervous sweat, the guy in charge of the panel had told him that the testimony of multiple witnesses bore out just how careful and methodical he was when it came to Bessie. Even Perkins had said he was competent, which Ryan still couldn't quite believe.

Although it would be weeks before the panel reported on its findings, Simon's statement that he'd seen Ryan conducting the inspection, together with the general testimony about his conscientiousness and the simple fact that anyone with malfeasance in mind could have accessed Bessie after Ryan had done the inspection, meant that it was impossible for them to find him at fault.

The guy who'd written his glowing report from the training course had also been consulted, and Ryan tried, so hard, not to *hate* the fact that he'd probably only been cleared because his ex-tutor was an old friend of the panel chairman. Even here, there was no escaping his father's world of wheels within wheels, where the only thing that counted was who you knew.

The chairman of the panel had concluded by saying they had no intention of recommending his suspension unless any inculpatory evidence came to light. Which was basically them covering their arses.

All three members of the board had shaken his hand before letting him leave, and the words of the guy in charge were still ringing in his ears. "Hell of a job you did there, stopping her." He couldn't remember the last time someone who didn't want something from him had praised him. Except Sam, but Sam had a spider as a pet, so what did he know?

Ryan was giddy with it suddenly—joy, and relief, and an uprush of warmth for the dorky guy next to him who was talking a mile a minute, waving his hands around to illustrate his point about braking systems and Ryan's tactics in slowing Bess.

Ryan could only think of one way to shut him up. He grabbed one of those wildly waving arms and swung Sam around to kiss him.

After the first moment of startled stillness, Sam kissed him back, just as enthusiastic as he always was. And kissing Sam felt so good that Ryan kept on doing it. Knowing they were in the street in the middle of the day, Ryan kept it PG-rated, simply settling his hands on Sam's hips to keep him close.

It turned out that PG-rated was enough for him, for now. He just wanted to be close to Sam, to somehow express the whole mixture of stuff inside him that he couldn't explain even to himself.

SAM

One minute Sam was expounding on just what a genius Ryan was; the next, Ryan was validating Sam's thesis by kissing him. It was a *much* better idea than talking, Sam promptly decided, as Ryan's kiss deepened slightly, just enough of a hint of tongue to have Sam chasing him back, wanting more.

They were interrupted by Ryan's phone ringing. It was probably as well, because when Ryan drew back with a muttered curse, Sam remembered that they were standing in the middle of the street where he lived. Which meant that any of the nosier neighbours—which was pretty well all of them—would have enjoyed a ringside seat.

Those thoughts fled at the look on Ryan's face as he read the incoming number. "What's wrong?"

Ryan started and looked up at him. "Nothing," he said. "I put a call in to my father earlier. I better take this."

"I'll go and put the kettle on," Sam said, wanting to give Ryan privacy to talk to his dad. He didn't think Ryan heard him, because he'd started speaking into the phone.

"Yeah, I know what you said, but I thought I should give you a heads-up," he was saying, and he sounded defensive. As if he'd done something wrong by contacting his own father.

Sam hesitated, just in case Ryan might prefer him to stay for moral support, but on seeing Ryan's whole attention was focused on the conversation he was holding, he went with his original plan. As he retreated down the pavement, he could hear Ryan's exasperated voice raised in a near-shout. "I didn't fucking well *do* anything."

Sam couldn't imagine ever swearing at Uncle Ken, let alone "putting a call in" to him and then having to wait to be called back. He glanced back as he unlocked his front door, and saw Ryan standing rigidly, one hand holding his phone to his ear and his other hand clenched into a fist.

RYAN

"I didn't fucking well *do* anything." One sentence, one fucking sentence, and his father had already got him so furious he could barely get the words out.

"That's what you always say, Ryan. It's always someone else's fault."

It stung, not least because of the truth in it. He plunged on before his father could end the call, because it sounded like he was seconds from hanging up. "Listen, there's something going on with the trust that runs Bessie—the train. Something stinks in their accounts, and someone tried to sabotage her and she nearly crashed."

"For God's sake, Ryan—you crashed the bloody train?"

"I *stopped* the bloody train from crashing. And I'm fine, thanks for asking."

"Clearly you are, or you wouldn't be calling me." The calm logic was maddeningly unanswerable, and Ryan's hand clenched on his phone. He just wanted his dad to *react* sometimes, to show some emotion instead of always being so fucking rational. As always with his father, it didn't matter what he wanted. "Why *are* you calling me about your latest screwup? You know it's in breach of our agreement." Their agreement into which he'd written a clause that, should Ryan break it, he'd forfeit both the flat and his ongoing monthly allowance. As if he didn't trust Ryan to honour anything without a threat.

"Because the Old Bill are going to be looking at the accounts and I thought I should warn you, given your donation." He should have left it at that, but anger and hurt wouldn't let him. "Obviously I'm just wasting your precious time," he added, a sneer in his voice.

"Oh, for God's sake, Ryan. Grow up."

He couldn't tell if the disgust in his father's voice was at his childishness—and Ryan couldn't understand how his father always made him revert to a sulky teenager—or at the fact Ryan had dragged him into yet another mess that was bound to hit the headlines.

"I didn't know." It spilled out of him, sounding desperate. "When I applied for the job here, when I asked you, I didn't *know*." As if that was any excuse. It was even more evidence of just how badly he'd failed—lack of due diligence on his part.

"You've clearly got access to the accounts." His father sidestepped his attempt to defend himself, or apologise, or whatever the hell that had been and went straight to the business issue at hand. Just the way he always did.

At least arranging to have the accounts couriered to him was safe, neutral territory. After that, his father ended the call.

"Fuck you too," Ryan said to the silent phone, but it didn't make him feel any better. Every time, every fucking time he spoke to his father was the same. He never listened. He never *heard* Ryan.

Fuck it. He blinked as the sun came out from behind the clouds, sudden brightness making his eyes sting. And then he remembered

Sam was waiting for him. Turning his phone off, Ryan headed for sanctuary.

SAM

Sam had just made the tea when Ryan came in through the open front door and picked up his mug from the kitchen counter. Obviously it hadn't been a long conversation.

"He's going to have a forensic accountant take a look at the books," Ryan said, taking a swig of tea and wrinkling his nose. Sam made it strong enough to stand a spoon up in, and Ryan liked his on the wimpy side of weak. Sam had forgotten that as he'd enthusiastically squeezed the teabag before fishing it out.

"Yeah? That's good of him, isn't it?" Sam said. He wasn't quite sure, because Ryan's tone was off, somehow.

"He needs to make sure no suggestion of wrongdoing can be attached to him if the accounts are going to be subject to scrutiny," Ryan said, and Sam blinked at the words, which sounded nothing like Ryan's normal style of speech. "He's covering his arse. For God's sake, Sam—this is like fucking wallpaper stripper."

He dumped the tea in the sink and put the kettle on again. Only he forgot to check it had enough water in and Sam lunged to switch it off before it burned out.

"For fuck's *sake*," Ryan snarled.

Sam concentrated on filling the kettle and putting it back on. He had the feeling anything he said right now would be the wrong thing.

Ryan took three times as long as necessary to make himself a mug of tea, and when he finally looked up at Sam after stirring the mug for about the fifteenth time, his eyes were no longer angry.

They just looked tired and a little sad. Sam wanted to hug him, but he was pretty sure Ryan wouldn't welcome that.

"Do you want something to eat?" he asked instead, because it was lunchtime after all.

Ryan shook his head and took his mug through to the sitting room. When Sam got there, he was sitting on the sofa, Sam's laptop already on his lap, booting up.

"We should see if the news about Bessie has hit your forum yet," he said. His grin was a wreck of its usual self, but Sam was willing to go along with it. Especially when Ryan got onto the forum and Sam's private message inbox was bursting at the seams. He usually got about one message a year, and that was spam.

"They all want to know if Bess is okay," Ryan said as he clicked through them, and then his eyes crinkled in a genuinely amused smile. "You know, I haven't seen *one* yet that wants to know if *you're* okay. Oh, I lied. Here we go—daryl234 is pleased you didn't get squished on the tracks and damage her wheels. That's nice of him, I suppose."

"How do they know I was involved?" Sam asked. News of Bess's dramatic near-miss had spread far and wide—even Melanie had heard about the old train, she said, when Sam had called to explain why he couldn't come into work that day—but he didn't see how anyone would know about his role in it.

Two minutes and a swift use of search engines later, Ryan turned the laptop towards Sam with a quizzical smile. Val, her hair a new shade of shocking pink, was on TV news, excitedly telling the interviewer *everything* she knew. It was based on the bare bones of what Sam had told her when he'd returned her keys, but wildly embellished.

"Sounds like she's got a bit of a case of hero-worship going on," Ryan said, after a mortified Sam had leaned over and closed the browser window. Val had been talking about Sam waving down the train using only the clothes he stood up in. She made him sound like some sort of stripper. "Am I going to have to warn her off?"

Sam choked at the concept that he and Val.... "*God*, no," he said. "I think she just likes the limelight."

He sat grinning like an idiot for the next hour while Ryan baited the people on the forum. Ryan had intended to warn Val off if she was interested in him. It meant he must *want* Sam. And it wasn't as if Sam hadn't *got* that from all the time they were spending together and the way Ryan had been with him ever since the hillside, more open, somehow, and something in him softer, but without Ryan ever *saying* anything, he wasn't sure where he stood.

Except for the part where he and Ryan were so comfortable together now that he knew this was much more than the casual hookup Ryan had suggested. They were friends who had wonderful sex, and he was beginning to believe they were more than that. Which was just as well, because he was head over heels in love with Ryan.

That afternoon, they went to see Mrs Johnson and asked to borrow her husband's papers. Ryan explained that they wanted to lend them to an accountant to go through because of some apparent anomalies, but made it clear that no blame was to be laid at the door of the trustees. Mrs Johnson was shocked into disconcerting silence by the revelation, but when she recovered the power of speech she agreed to lend them the papers just so long as she got them all back.

While she busied herself getting them from wherever they were kept, refusing any help, they sat on the high-backed formal couch in the sitting room, drinking tea out of dainty porcelain cups and waging a silent but deadly battle over the last piece of shortbread. Sam had swiped it from under Ryan's nose, but soon found out that Ryan didn't take defeat well. He had Sam pinned on the cushions of the couch, convulsed with barely suppressed laughter as he found that ticklish spot again, when Mrs Johnson came back into the room.

"Really, Sam," she said. "You're too big for that sort of behaviour now."

Ryan's triumphant grin above him turned positively filthy. He very deliberately nudged his crotch against Sam's, reminding him just how big he was, before sitting up straight and smiling innocently at Mrs Johnson while Sam blushed so hard he must have turned scarlet.

But when Ryan broke the shortbread he had so deviously purloined in two and gave Sam half, Sam forgot everything except how much he loved Mrs Johnson's shortbread and Ryan Saunders.

RYAN

Ryan arranged for a courier to pick up the files from Sam's house. He'd need to sign when they were collected, so he had to hang round at Sam's the rest of the afternoon. Not that he actually wanted to do anything else, let alone go back to that sterile flat with the snooty neighbours. Sam's house was a bit shabby and dated, but it was comfortable. And most importantly, it had Sam.

Also, it turned out, Mabel.

"Fucking *hell*, Sam—I thought you said she was only there at night." Ryan knew he was breathing hard as he stood in the living room doorway glaring at Sam, but for fuck's sake—he'd gone to use the bathroom and that fucking *monster* had been lurking in the shower.

Sam had just returned from dealing with Mabel, his jaw set mutinously at Ryan's perfectly reasonable suggestion that if death and dismemberment weren't options, he should take her down the road so she'd make her home in someone else's bathroom, when the doorbell rang.

Ryan sighed—he was *never* going to get to the bathroom at this rate—and went to sign the courier's paperwork. Only to find a young blond guy standing there without a piece of paper in sight. Shocked recognition dawned on the guy's face as he saw Ryan, and for an instant Ryan wondered if this was someone he'd once screwed. He had a bit of a job remembering, seeing as most of the time it wasn't their face he'd been looking at.

"I'm looking for Sam Chancellor," the guy said.

Sam heard him and came to the door, curious.

"Matt Deede, from the five o'clock news," the blond started, and Ryan grabbed the door and shut it firmly in his face.

Sam turned to him. "Why did you do that? That was rude."

"Believe me, Sam, you don't want anything to do with the press. I thought you'd have learned that by now."

Sam flinched, and Ryan felt like a prick. "Seriously, they'll twist anything you say and before you know it *you'll* become the story, not Bessie. Just ignore them and they'll go away."

Ignoring Matt Deede didn't make him go away. He was knocking on the door again and calling Sam's name. Ryan pulled Sam back into the living room and tried to concentrate on winding up Nobby on the forum. But as the afternoon wore on, there were increasingly frequent knocks both on the door and the window of the front room, the one that looked like a dining room which Sam didn't seem to use. It felt like they were being laid to siege. And then Ryan's phone rang.

"Sod it," he said as he ended the call. "The courier's outside." He looked at Sam and shook his head in resignation. "You might as well answer a few questions, let them get their photos, and they'll bugger off. Just don't talk about *anything* that isn't Bessie."

Ryan shouldered his way through the throng that had assembled outside Sam's house, so clearly unwilling to answer a single question of the many fired at him that the pack swiftly turned their attention to Sam. Ryan felt bad leaving Sam to their tender mercies as he dealt with the courier, but the sooner his father got these papers, the better. He didn't trust small-town coppers to find their arses with both hands, let alone read and understand complicated accounts, and his father employed only the best. If there was anything wrong with these, even a single digit that hadn't been carried, it would be found.

Papers safely dispatched, Ryan found that Sam was explaining the finer points of Westinghouse's triple-valve braking system to his audience. The dazed expressions on the journalists' seasoned faces had Ryan grinning. It wasn't that Sam was ignoring their questions—it seemed he thought he could answer their questions better if they understood the whole picture.

"This is a bit of a turn up for the books, isn't it, Ryan—you, of all people, getting an honest job?"

The voice was naggingly familiar, and when he looked at the woman smirking at him, he recognised her as the stupid blonde cow who used to write one of the tabloid gossip columns. She'd always had it in for him.

"Almost as surprising as you being a proper reporter at last," he said, and wrapped his hand around Sam's wrist. "You've had my boyfriend long enough. I'm taking him inside."

Sam allowed himself to be tugged back through the door, which Ryan firmly locked behind them, and pressed up against the wall. "Boyfriend?" he asked, with the beginning of a delighted smile in his eyes.

Ryan had only said it so that the press would leave Sam alone and concentrate their sharp words on him, because the thought of Ryan Saunders having a relationship for longer than it took to have sex was about as likely as Simon breaking into a Shakespearean monologue. But seeing the happiness in Sam, the trust and—and fondness shining from his eyes, Ryan knew his subconscious had betrayed him.

It had never really been about getting the reporters' attention off Sam. It had been about making sure everyone knew Sam was his.

"Yeah," he said, and leaned in closer, his lips a few inches away from Sam's. "You have a problem with that?"

Sam surged forward to kiss him, nearly head-butting him in his eagerness, and Ryan had his answer.

SAM

Sam knew he was going to wake up soon, but he didn't want to. He wanted to continue in this wonderful world where he and Ryan Saunders were boyfriends. He didn't even have to go to work this week, because his super-smart *boyfriend* had suggested that the shop wouldn't like being invaded by paparazzi trying to get a shot of Sam stocking the condom shelf. Or, knowing his luck, the feminine hygiene shelf. Melanie spoke to Beaky for him, who thankfully agreed, and he was allowed to take a week's leave.

Bess was back in her shed, but at the moment she was in the hands of Perkins and the maintenance company. Sam couldn't see how it could take *that* long to check for any other damage, but he supposed all the open questions over who might be responsible for the sabotage meant that she was basically on lockdown until that was resolved. And while he hoped it wouldn't be too long before Bess was running again, the upside of the situation was that he and Ryan spent all day, every day together.

The first day they'd had a few reporters and photographers in their faces when they left the house, but Ryan was completely unfazed by it, not to mention downright rude to them, so Sam just tagged along in his wake, smiling nervously without saying anything. The media soon realised there was no real story here, not once the first *Troubled heir to the Saunders fortune redeems himself* stories had hit the press, and they melted away.

The next few days were the most perfect of Sam's life. Ryan took him out on the back of his motorbike, and after the first minutes of mind-numbing terror at how the bike tipped around corners and how he kept sliding on the seat and hadn't Ryan heard of *speed limits*, Sam realised this was actually pretty awesome, swooping around the curving roads high above the town, holding tight to Ryan and smiling fit to bust.

It seemed like it was Ryan's mission in life to terrify Sam, because no sooner had he got used to being on the back of Ryan's bike than Ryan took him into a shop. One of *those* shops, where it was so dimly lit Sam could scarcely see in front of his nose, where there were about three items of clothing on display, and where thin, fashionable young women looked down their noses at him.

"Jeans," Ryan said. "You're getting some."

"But I—" Sam gestured at the jeans he was wearing, which had years of wear left in them.

"You're going to make me cry. You have got the most perfect arse known to man, and you wear *those*?"

"But..." Sam looked around helplessly, because he couldn't even see any jeans for sale here.

Ryan sauntered to the back of the shop. Straining his eyes in the gloom, Sam could see that the rear wall held a series of little cubbyholes, each of which contained a pair of folded up jeans. It was a million miles away from Braddons, where the jeans were on hangers, arranged by size. He couldn't understand how they were organised here, but Ryan picked out a couple of pairs without hesitation before herding him to the changing rooms.

It seemed easiest to go along with Ryan, so Sam obediently tried them on. Once he'd done so, he found himself staring at his reflection in the mirror. He didn't look like Sam any more. The soft, dark-wash denim clung to his thighs and, well, other places. He looked kind of like Ryan did in his jeans. He wasn't sure if he liked it, but he thought he might.

"Come on then, let's have a look."

Sam suspected the only thing that had stopped Ryan coming in with him had been the lack of space in the changing room. He ventured out to where Ryan was waiting and promptly decided he *did* like these jeans, because Ryan looked like he was about to have a heart attack. In a good way. And then he decided to check the fit of Sam's jeans and his inside leg measurement and which side he dressed, and all sorts of other things that Sam was *sure* weren't necessary but which he wasn't going to protest about given that it meant Ryan's hands were all over him.

He was still wearing the jeans when they left the shop, with another two pairs in a bag at his side. He'd been appalled at how much they cost, but he could afford it and, more importantly, the way Ryan was lagging about three steps behind him on the way back to his flat made him think it was money well spent. Especially when, the instant they were through the door, Ryan's hands were on his arse. Sam wasn't above giving a little wiggle, and Ryan groaned into his ear as he pressed up close behind him.

"Tease," he said, but it didn't sound like he was complaining. His cock most certainly wasn't, because it was pressing against Sam and there was something to be said for close-fitting jeans made of soft denim, because he could clearly feel how hard Ryan was as he rubbed against him.

They stumbled together into Ryan's bedroom, where Sam's new jeans hit the floor pretty damn quickly, and then Ryan was working him open before sliding inside, hot and slick and *perfect*. There was no teasing—he was fucking into Sam until Sam came all over the quilt beneath him, involuntary sounds escaping him in the flat that was silent except for the sound of flesh against flesh and Ryan's panting. Ryan shuddered into him and was finally still, groaning out his pleasure in a deep, throaty sound that had Sam wanting to come all over again as his arms gave out and he toppled forward onto the bed.

As he came back slowly to himself, he found Ryan was sprawled on top of him, his body heavy and warm and the best thing in the world. Sam didn't want him to move, and from the protesting sound Ryan made when he dealt with the condom, he wasn't alone in that. Throwing it in the direction of the bin—and Sam had been relieved to discover what good aim Ryan had—he flopped back on the bed beside Sam. Late-afternoon light slanted through the window onto Ryan's angled jaw and the beginnings of stubble that dusted it. He looked like all of Sam's dreams come true.

"Fuck, I'm starving," he said.

Sam crashed back to reality. It turned out reality was even better than his dreams, because Ryan was *Ryan*—not some perfect figure who Sam could only disappoint, but a guy who swore too much, who liked his tea to consist of hot water and milk, and who never picked up his dirty socks, judging by the number scattered around the bedroom.

As Sam looked around the room, his heart jolted and his stomach turned over—there was a packing crate in the corner of the room. He was sure it hadn't been there the last time he'd been here, when Ryan had been hurt.

"Ryan," he said, and his voice sounded strange. "Are you—what—" Bereft of words, he nodded towards the crate.

Ryan twisted to see what Sam was looking at. "Oh," he said.

He lay silently for a minute, while Sam tried to remember how to breathe. Of course it had all been too good to be true. Of course it had, but somehow he'd believed it.

"Are you leaving?" he asked at last, because Ryan wasn't saying anything further.

Ryan swallowed, then he turned to face Sam. They were only inches away, but it felt like miles. "I was going to," he said. "I was losing my job, and there wasn't anything to keep me here. At least that's what I thought. Now..." And he paused for so long that Sam's heart was about to pound out of his chest. "Now there is," he said at last, and leaned in to press a short, sweet kiss on Sam's lips. "I guess I'm staying."

"I love you," Sam blurted out, his voice scratchy and ugly.

Before he could wonder if he'd said the wrong thing, Ryan pulled him close and held him, his heart beating harder than usual as he buried his face in Sam's hair. He didn't say it back, but the way he held Sam meant he didn't need to.

Chapter Sixteen

RYAN

The days that followed were pretty sweet. Cardale was still a one-horse town that was about thirty years behind the rest of the country, but Ryan was learning that it wasn't all bad. At least, not when seen through Sam's eyes.

They spent most of their time at Sam's. Every so often they'd open the door to find a container of fruit or vegetables sitting on the doorstep. That was weird, but Sam seemed to like it. Even the fact that they got stared at when they went out together didn't spoil things. Ryan had never given a toss what anyone thought of him, and Sam didn't seem to notice. At least, not until one afternoon when Sam froze in his tracks at the sound of an imperious voice behind them.

"Samuel."

The name was so unfamiliar that Ryan had no idea it was directed at Sam until he saw the look on Sam's face. He turned around to see just what could instil such fear in him and found a little old lady moving towards them, a very determined glint in her eye.

Something about her tugged at his memory, and when Sam's shoulders hunched and his Adam's apple bobbed nervously, it came into focus—it was the woman who'd been scolding Sam outside the station the day they'd met.

"Well," she said as she reached them, looking them both up and down. "You've been rather busy lately, haven't you?"

"Um, yes?" Sam said uncertainly. Ryan grinned at the squeak in his voice.

"And you must be Ryan." The woman turned her attention to him and the grin died on his face. Her penetrating gaze gave him the distinct impression he had been judged and found wanting.

"And you are?" he asked, without even trying to stop the way his lip curled. He'd been brought up properly once, but hell if he was going to let some old bat look at him like he was a piece of dirt on Sam's shoe.

"Diana Verity." Her voice as precise and controlled as her stance. "How do you do."

He nodded slightly in response because Sam knew her, so blowing her off completely would probably upset him. But he kept staring back at her, silently letting her know he was just as unimpressed as she was. So maybe she thought he wasn't good enough for Sam, but it was none of her damn business.

As he met her keen gaze, he kept his hand firmly in the back pocket of Sam's jeans. It had been there for the past ten minutes, enjoying the warm curve of Sam's arse, and he had no intention of changing the situation just because she disapproved of him.

"Is that Bess?" Sam's question broke the awkward standoff.

Mrs Verity's attention returned to Sam, and with an indulgent smile she handed over the *Cardale Evening Chronicle* that had been lying in her wicker shopping basket. Sure enough, there was a big picture of Bessie on the front page. That wasn't all—there was also the picture of Ryan from Bessie's website, his driver's cap at the perfect rakish angle as he eye-fucked the camera, and a photo of Sam that defied description.

"How *old* are you there?" Ryan demanded. "Eight?"

Sam flushed. "Sixteen," he said defiantly.

Yeah, right. On a second, more thorough look at the photo, Ryan might have put Sam at twelve. He was stick thin, his shoulders were hunched in an all-too-familiar way and his tense attempt at a grin seemed only to draw attention to the braces on his teeth. With the rat's nest on his head added to the mix, sixteen-year-old Sam was a tragedy of epic proportions.

Except, as Ryan looked a little longer, he could still see Sam in the dark eyes that looked so on edge. He wished he'd got to know Sam earlier and been able to save him from the bullying he must have gone through, looking like that and being gay and a trainspotter into the bargain.

But even as Ryan thought it, he knew that without the body Sam now had, Ryan would never have stopped long enough to look beneath, and God—what he'd have missed. What *everyone* had missed, except perhaps this old woman, because she had her hand on Sam's arm and her expression was so soft that she looked like a different person from the one who'd been glaring at him.

"Ken was tremendously proud of you," she said, with a little squeeze to Sam's arm. "And if he knew you'd saved Bess, there'd have been no stopping him."

Sam's throat worked again and his eyes looked suspiciously damp. Ryan stepped in to rescue him.

"Bloody hell," he said, snatching the paper from Sam and waving that terrible photo around just in case anyone had missed it.

"So on top of everything else, half the town now thinks I'm a cradle-snatcher?"

It was Mrs Verity who answered, her words slow and thoughtful, yet very sure. "I suspect that you don't give a fig what most of the town thinks of you, Ryan. Only those who matter."

Ryan was still trying to work out how he was supposed to respond to that when she reached out to retrieve her slightly crumpled evening paper and bade them both farewell.

"Where the *hell* did they dig up that picture of you?" he asked Sam, who was gazing after Mrs Verity.

The slight sadness lingering in Sam's face was chased away by mortification. "Dawn," he said. "From work," he added when Ryan still stared at him, none the wiser. "We went to school together, so she must have found it from somewhere and given it to her dad to use."

"You should sue," Ryan said automatically, but he couldn't really keep his mind on what he was saying because as he looked at Sam, he could still see that uncertain, unhappy-looking kid in the photo. He knew with everything in him that he never wanted Sam to look like that again.

But even that newfound knowledge didn't stop him from plotting Mabel's demise. When Sam found Ryan on his phone one evening, searching to find out how long spiders lived, his face was a picture of disappointment. "You really don't like her, do you?"

"No." He didn't see why he should have to apologise for that. She—*it*—was a damn *spider*. And if a little part of him felt he should try to like her because she seemed to have been Sam's only company since his uncle had died, that part withered and disappeared whenever he saw her lurking malevolently in the shower, ready to scuttle at him on long, black, hairy legs at the first sign of fear.

They began to stay at Ryan's more often so that Ryan could go to the bathroom in the night without risking a heart attack, and Sam could have a lie-in in the mornings if he wanted, rather than having to get up to deal with Mabel before Ryan could shower. That turned out to be a tactical error on Ryan's part, because Sam really did love his bed. To the point where he never wanted to leave it before about ten o'clock.

It turned out that the only way to wake Sam up properly was by morning sex. Perhaps it wasn't that much of a tactical error.

It was getting towards the end of Sam's week off work and they hadn't long been out of bed, despite the fact it was nearly midday, when Ryan's intercom buzzed. A courier needed him to sign for a delivery. Ryan let him into the building, and when the guy turned up at the front door to his flat, he was carrying Mrs Johnson's box of files.

"Has your dad finished with them, then?" Sam asked, crouching down to open the box and check all the files were safely there.

Ryan shrugged jerkily. "How would I know?"

Sam's mouth opened slightly as he glanced up, but then he busied himself looking through the files. He was trying to cover, but the look on his face said what he so carefully didn't—how messed up it was that Ryan's father wouldn't even text him to let him know the status of things. Yeah, well. They'd made a deal, and part of that had been no further contact. One of the reasons his father was so successful was that he always honoured the deals he made.

Thankfully the intercom went again before things could get any more awkward. The delivery guy must have forgotten something, because it wasn't as if anyone ever visited. Which Ryan liked, by the way. But it wasn't the delivery guy; it was the head of the board of trustees, Harold Matthews.

Ryan buzzed him in, careful to wipe any expression from his face before he turned to look at Sam. Somehow over the past few days of being with Sam, he'd managed not to think about it, and this, now, hit him like a punch in the gut. It didn't matter what the accident board had said. The trustees wouldn't want someone with his history driving their precious train. His chest was hollow all of a sudden, and his head seemed very far away from his feet.

"Should I go?" Sam asked, looking uneasy.

Ryan opened his mouth to say yes because he didn't want anyone to witness his humiliation. But then he saw behind Sam to that watercolour of Bess that he'd bought. When Sam had found it in the pile of junk in Ryan's living room, he'd insisted they hang it on the wall above the mantelpiece. Somehow that one act had made the place feel different. More like *his*. And they'd started to empty the packing crates together, as if Ryan was moving into the flat and the town and his life.

Even without driving Bessie, this was his life now, here in Cardale. With Sam. It gave him more than he'd ever had. *Sam* gave him more than he'd ever had.

"Stay," he said.

Sam nodded, pretending not to notice that the word had sounded a little hoarse. He sat down on the sofa, making an obvious effort not to fidget while Ryan let Matthews in. Just the sight of him in the suit that did nothing to disguise the belly he was carrying from all those fine meals and drinks on expenses had Ryan's hackles on end. He'd spent too much time around self-important dicks like this, dicks who ran the country behind the scenes by virtue of who they knew. He never wanted anything to do with them again.

But under his air of arrogant superiority, Matthews was ill at ease. Ryan didn't know if it was because he'd just entered a den of gay vice—Sam's shirt was wrongly buttoned and his bedhead always looked like sex hair to Ryan—or if it was because he didn't like telling people to their face that they were fired.

Ryan refused to offer him a seat, so Matthews stood in the middle of the room. His jowls wobbled slightly as he cleared his throat before speaking. And maybe Ryan was petty for noticing that, but he'd take anything he could get to make himself feel superior over the wanker who was going to take Bessie away from him.

"I'm very sorry to have to inform you that Daniel Cleaver was arrested this morning and charged with a number of offences relating to fraud and criminal damage with intent to endanger life," Matthews said.

"Good." Ryan was filled with vicious satisfaction.

Matthews shifted his weight slightly. "I understand that he may have been subjecting you to improper pressure," he said to Ryan. "The trustee board would like to apologise for that."

Ryan stared at him, speechless in shock, before marshalling his thoughts. He was *not* going to let this dick dismantle his defences before delivering the final, fatal blow. He wouldn't be caught like that any more.

"Yeah, well," he said, and almost made it sound like he didn't care.

"We've taken steps to ensure nothing like this can ever happen again," Matthews said, with evidently no intention of disclosing just what those steps were to nobodies like Ryan and Sam. "In the meantime, we have the green light from the accident board and the maintenance company to keep operating the engine, so we'll be opening the line again the day after tomorrow."

He looked at Ryan expectantly. Ryan looked back at him. He didn't have an idea in hell what he was supposed to say.

"I take it that's not going to be a problem," Matthews said at last, a slight frown on his face informing Ryan that it better *not* be a problem.

Ryan moistened his lips. It couldn't be what it sounded like. He knew better than to believe it might be true, but somewhere inside him hope was beginning to grow. Hope that was suddenly so fierce that he couldn't quite breathe.

"Mr Saunders, the accident board informed us in no uncertain terms that your skill, together with Mr Chancellor's actions, prevented a terrible accident. We would like to make a small presentation to you both tomorrow, with a photographer from the *Cardale Evening Chronicle* present, before we start operating again on Wednesday morning. I take it that's acceptable?"

"I—" The words stuck in his throat, which was probably as well because he didn't know what the fuck he was going to say but it would probably involve lots of swearing because fucking *hell*—they wanted him to *stay*?

He looked at Sam, who was leaning forward, excitement all over his face, and it began to dawn on him that this really was true. He wasn't getting sacked. He'd get to keep driving Bessie.

"That's fine," he said at last, in a level, colourless tone. He wasn't giving that dick any satisfaction, especially as he was sure they were only keeping him because the first lot of stories to hit the media had been based on Val's account, which was based on Sam's, which inevitably had painted Ryan as some sort of hero. The trust would look bad if they got rid of him now.

It was only when they'd shaken hands and Matthews had left, promising to let them have details of arrangements for the following day, that he realised what he'd just agreed to.

"The *Cardale* sodding *Chronicle*," he said. "What the hell?"

"I know," Sam said, "but firstly, it means everyone who saw that first story will see this one, and secondly—who cares? Ryan, Bess is running again, and you're driving her, and they're giving you an *award*."

"Not just me—you're getting something as well to reward you for getting naked around Bess," he pointed out. "Maybe they didn't think that one through."

The laughter in Sam's face brightened the room. His eyes were shining with excitement and he reminded Ryan of how that little boy Josh had looked when he'd ridden on Bessie—full to the brim with sheer joy.

Ryan felt the same way. The only thing was, it wasn't Bessie causing that feeling in him. It was Sam. Sam, who was in his arms, kissing him, laughing and happy.

Chapter Seventeen

SAM

Sam had thought the presentation would involve just him, Ryan and Simon, with Matthews and the photographer. He was gobsmacked to walk into Bess's shed and find a crowd of people.

As well as the entire board of trustees and their guests, there was Marlene, and Val, and Ritchie and Amit, and even Mrs Verity, who seemed to be accompanying one of the trustees. She smiled at them both as they arrived, but to Sam's relief didn't come to talk to them. Unlike Mrs Johnson, who cornered them immediately. She was representing her husband, she informed Sam in a voice that quivered slightly. Of course she was pleased to be here to see Sam recognised for what he'd done, but the trust had been her husband's passion, not hers. He would have been terribly shocked by what had happened, as they all were, of course. Who would have *thought* that Daniel Cleaver had a gambling addiction, let alone that he'd do such terrible things to pay for it? Even though there'd always been something about him that she couldn't quite like. Thankfully, Matthews showed up at that point to take Ryan and Sam away and introduce them to a bewildering number of people.

In the centre of all the fuss stood Bess, vast and regal. Sam's heart ached thinking of what might have happened to her. He was so busy drinking in her beauty that he almost missed the moment when Matthews asked him to step forward. He realised suddenly that people had formed a loose semicircle around Bess and that Matthews was looking at him expectantly.

His cheeks were hot as he made his way over to Matthews. They got even warmer when everyone started clapping and Val wolf-whistled. Matthews shook his hand and gave him a silver tankard and the photographer took a whole load of pictures. After that, Matthews said nice things about his observational skills, quick thinking and resourcefulness, things which Sam didn't really take in because he was too busy looking at the tankard. It had a picture of Bess engraved on it and the date of the incident and his name, along with a short citation that had some of the same words Matthews was using.

His ears pricked up, however, when Matthews got to the part about him now having the same access to Bess as the members of the board, which meant he could ride on her for free whenever he wished and that, with enough notice and the agreement of Bess's crew, he could occasionally ride on the footplate when she went out. Beyond words, he pumped Matthews's hand, grinning around wildly until he found Ryan. Ryan's smile probably looked like a smirk to anyone else, but Sam could see the fondness in it.

Then it was his turn to applaud madly when Ryan was presented with his own tankard and commended for his skill and courage in staying with Bess even at the risk of his own life. Simon too was called forward, and Sam's hands had never been so sore.

After it was over, there were glasses of champagne, which Sam found he didn't like very much, and little snacks on silver trays, and he wondered how the trust could afford this if Cleaver had taken so much money from them. But when he saw Matthews home in on the reporter from the *Chronicle*, ensuring her glass was kept filled, he realised it wasn't really about them. It was about getting the best publicity possible for Bess.

Bess, whose silent presence loomed over everything. Even Mrs Johnson looked interested as she listened to Mr Perkins, who was giving a guided tour to most of the guests. At any other time Sam would have been desperate to join them and hear exactly what Mr Perkins had to say, but he was perfectly happy where he was because Ryan was beside him. His hand was brushing Sam's arse, the way it always seemed to now that he had his new jeans, and he was watching the circus around them with a smile tugging at the corners of his lips.

"Who'd have thought it?" he said quietly to Sam.

When he turned to look at Ryan, Sam thought he had never seen him so peaceful and contented.

"I know, right?" Sam's face ached with the force of his smile. "I mean, I get to ride on Bess's footplate. Can you *imagine*?" Lost in the magic of that thought, he didn't care that his voice came out sounding a little high-pitched and breathless.

But even that promise didn't compare to the moment later that evening when everyone else had gone, and Ryan and Sam were alone with Bess. Ryan's keys had been returned to him, so they could stay as long as they liked. Ryan had turned off some of the harsh overhead lights, leaving ones at the far end of the shed, which cast just enough light to have Bess gleaming softly.

And then he'd come up behind Sam and slid his arms around his waist, reaching up slightly to prop his chin on Sam's shoulder.

They fitted together perfectly like this, just like Bess did with her carriages.

"Sometimes I used to do this when everyone else left," Ryan said against his ear. "Just stay back a while and be with her."

Sam could understand that impulse. He leaned back into Ryan's hold, loving his warmth and strength, and the comfort of his closeness. He had the feeling that now he was allowed in the engine shed—under strict supervision, Matthews had been careful to stress, and Ryan had given an extremely wolfish-looking grin, as if he was imagining just what that might entail—he and Ryan might end most of their days like this. Together, with Bess. He couldn't want for anything more.

RYAN

As Ryan looked at Bessie, he thought of the things she'd seen, the ways in which the world had changed around her, and the fact that she kept going, strong, immutable and beautiful. He loved that hunk of iron and steel, the one that had led him to this dead-end town and had brought Sam Chancellor into his life.

Sam was standing in reverent silence as he drank in the experience of being alone with Bessie, but his hands rested lightly on Ryan's arms where they wrapped around his waist—evidence that, even in the presence of his first love, he hadn't forgotten Ryan. As Ryan pressed a brief kiss on the warmth of his neck and saw the corner of Sam's mouth raise in a smile, he remembered all over again that Bessie wasn't the only one who Sam loved.

Sam turned in his arms, his eyes warm and tender, an expression so new to Ryan it still stole his breath away. It was everything

Ryan had ever wanted and Sam was offering it to him freely. Ryan wanted to give him the same in return.

"I love you," he said.

The joy in Sam's face was like the moment Bessie got to the top of that long climb and was on the roof of the world—open and beautiful and perfect.

They kissed as Bessie watched over them. It was long and slow and sweet, like summer days that would never end. And Ryan knew that he'd finally found where he belonged.

JOY LYNN FIELDING

About the author

joy lives in a small English market town, where she indulges her passions for vintage aircraft, horse riding and gardening (though not all at the same time).

Joy talks a lot about the fascinating facts she discovers during her research for books. Thankfully, she has a very patient Labrador who has a gift for looking interested in what she's saying while he waits for the food to arrive.

Contact

Email: joy@joylynnfielding.com

Other books by Joy Lynn Fielding

The Red Dragon of Oxford

Dragons aren't real. Or so I *used* to think.

Oxford isn't exactly what I'd imagined. Sure, the colleges are romantic, and everyone is brilliant enough to trigger my impostor syndrome. I expected *that*.

The dragon, however, was a *big* surprise.

I saw him on my first day. The beautiful beast spoke to me, then disappeared. I've been looking for him ever since.

When I'm not on a wild dragon chase, I spend my time in the library. I'd like to think I'm only there to study, but who am I kidding?

I'm there for *him*.

Rufus Mortimer is the world's hottest librarian. He's strict, enigmatic, and sexy. He makes me feel things I've never felt before.

But he has a secret. One that could destroy *everything*.

So now, all I have to do is find a dragon, earn my doctorate, and try not to let my new romance burn my life to the ground. Easy, right?

I wish...

A Star to Sail By

On the dangerous high seas, there is nothing more precious than trust...

Billy loves the freedom he has as a pirate, where no man is his master. But when his captain tasks him with guarding an abducted naval officer, he starts questioning everything he *thought* he ever needed.

Crispin Merrick wants nothing more than to command a ship in the Royal Navy. Even though the war has ended and he's been stripped of his duties, he still dreams of naval glory. But being kidnapped and held captive by a pirate with the face of an angel and the soul of a scoundrel makes him wonder if it's finally time for some *new* dreams.

Can these polar opposites overcome their differences in time to survive what their enemies (and the treacherous seas) have in store for them?

Only if they can trust in each other—and in love—when the time comes...

Printed in Great Britain
by Amazon

53096711R00131